Snowflakes, Silver and Secrets

Seaview Stables Adventures

The PONY With No NAME

The Mystery at Stormy Point

Snowflakes, Silver and Secrets

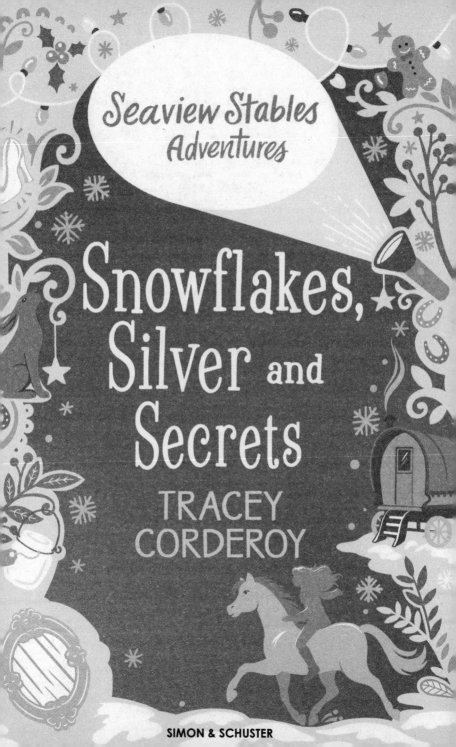

Seaview Stables
Adventures

Snowflakes, Silver and Secrets

TRACEY CORDEROY

SIMON & SCHUSTER

First published in Great Britain in 2019 by Simon & Schuster UK Ltd
A CBS COMPANY

Copyright © 2019 Tracey Corderoy Ltd

1 3 5 7 9 10 8 6 4 2

Simon & Schuster UK Ltd
1st Floor, 222 Gray's Inn Road
London
WC1X 8HB

www.simonandschuster.co.uk
www.simonandschuster.com.au
www.simonandschuster.co.in

Simon & Schuster Australia, Sydney
Simon & Schuster India, New Delhi

A CIP catalogue record for this book is
available from the British Library.

PB ISBN 978-1-4711-7045-4
eBook ISBN 978-1-4711-7046-1

Typeset in Bembo by M Rules
Printed and bound by CPI Group (UK) Ltd, Croydon, CR0 4YY

MIX
Paper from
responsible sources
FSC® C020471
FSC
www.fsc.org

*For Charlotte,
who has always loved Christmas ...*

Chapter 1

'It's snowing!' cried Bryony. 'I *saw* it! A flake — floating down past Red's ears!'

She tickled her bay pony behind his left ear and Red gave a delighted little whinny. He loved to be tickled just there and Bryony knew it.

'You saw that snowflake too, right, Red?' She smiled, gently bringing him to a halt outside the caves. It was a freezing Monday morning and the beach was deserted, even though it looked more beautiful than ever. The sand twinkled with early-morning frost and the tumbling waves were a dark steely-blue.

Bryony's friends gathered around on their ponies, and her twin brother, Josh, who much preferred wheels to hooves, pedalled over on his bike. The Super Six, as the friends called themselves, had ridden the whole stretch of beach. They'd even braved it into the deep gloomy caves, seeking out mystery and adventure. Everyone was excited. School had finished and Christmas was just five days away. But snow would make everything even more magical, so Bryony had been on the lookout for it since last Friday!

The ponies stood nuzzling each other playfully, their warm breath misting the air. Red's ears were pricked up and his big brown eyes bright. Bryony loved how friendly he was. All the ponies (except Piggy) were stabled at Seaview, which was why they'd become such great pals. Their owners were now Bryony's best friends too, and they'd planned lots of great hacks over the Christmas holidays.

'Hey, Em,' grinned Bryony, 'lucky old Piggy. We all need a warm coat like his today!'

Emma smiled. 'Yes. Piggy's made for winter!'

Emma's pony was a roly-poly little Shetland who looked like an overgrown guinea pig. He had a very thick coat and a long shaggy mane, both of which had a tendency to tangle. Emma tried her best to keep him knot-free, and Bryony helped. But Piggy didn't seem that bothered. As long as he could snack and nap he was happy!

Princess Perla, standing just beside Piggy, couldn't have looked more different. A tall, beautiful palomino mare, her coat was as shiny as a unicorn's! Her owner, Alice, loved her looking neat, although Princess P preferred daring hillside climbs – and mud.

Next was Daffodil, a young Welsh Connemara cross and the joker of the group. She stole hats off heads and swiped washing off lines. A cute dapple grey with a tufty coat and fluffy ears, Daffy *knew* she was lovely too! Hari, who'd only fairly recently got her, might tut at Daffy's antics, but was clearly already smitten.

Tornado was a little way off from the gang. He was a timid black gelding who belonged to Bryony's brother's best friend, Finn. Tor was currently backing away from a crab who'd suddenly scuttled from a rock pool. He was curious, but also really liked routine – so best avoid surprises or Tor could bolt off faster than a tornado!

And then there was sweet, gentle Red. Red was

everything Bryony could want. His rich bay coat was the colour of toffee apples in the morning sunshine and his midnight-black mane and tail looked shinier than ever. The cutest little kiss curl tumbled over his eyes and the small white star shape between them.

Bryony leaned forward and patted him gently, breathing in his delicious cinnamon scent. Every pony had their own special smell and Red's reminded Bryony of Christmas – so perfect for this time of year! Being his owner still sometimes felt like a dream.

Red's ear gave a flick and he whinnied brightly. He was full of beans today. 'What?' laughed Bryony. 'You *did* see that snowflake. I knew it!'

'Wishful thinking!' grinned Hari, flicking back her long black plait. Hari might be straight-talking but she was such a loyal friend and always there for Bryony when it counted.

'But it does feel cold enough,' Alice added kindly. She *always* thought the best. Her wavy blonde hair twirled down from her riding hat, not a single curl out of place. Bryony longed for neat hair like that. But even in the frost, Bryony's auburn frizz stayed as tightly curled as a dog whelk!

'Thanks, Alice,' said Bryony. 'But maybe Hari's right.'

Then Finn examined the sky too.

'No, I reckon snow's definitely on the cards.'

'Really?' Bryony smiled, and Finn nodded back.

'So yesterday I got this book from the library, and—'

''Course you did!' Hari chipped in.

Finn devoured books like Piggy hoovered hay!

'Anyway, this book was about the weather,' went on Finn, 'and it said that *low* stratus clouds generally bring rain, while higher stratus clouds are associated with *snow*. And the ones in the sky now aren't terribly low-hanging, see?'

Bryony squinted up. She didn't really see. Clouds were just *clouds*, she'd always thought.

'Anyway, Bry,' interrupted Josh. 'Let's keep moving before I turn into an icicle!'

Shivering, he led the way off the beach, pushing his bike up the steep sandy slope as the others followed behind. The plan was to head to Bluebell Wood next as it always looked so beautiful in the frost.

Bryony's fingers were stinging like mad as Red

trotted her up onto the pier. The sharp sea breeze had made them stiff and numb even though she was wearing thick gloves. She hoped Red wasn't feeling the cold too much. But judging by the spring in his step and pricked-up ears, he was fine.

They continued along the pier, past some kiosks which were closed, then headed down Smuggler's Lane. This was the first of a tangle of little lanes weaving out from Brook Dale's seafront to the fields, woods and meadows beyond.

The lane was narrow so they got into pairs. Bryony and Alice went out in front, then came Hari and Emma, with Finn and Josh bringing up the rear.

'Oh, that's better, Red!' Bryony smiled, and Red whinnied back brightly. It felt instantly more sheltered here with the trees and thick woody hedges acting as a windbreak.

There were so many lovely things to see too: busy little squirrels bounding about, berries that shimmered with frost and the silvery brook skipping along beside them.

Red nosed out in front as they took the next bend.

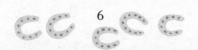

'Steady, boy,' called Bryony. For there in the lane was another pony trotting towards them.

It was a tall powerful palomino with a beautifully glossy coat. And sitting very upright on the pony's back was Bryony's arch-enemy, Georgina Brook.

It was clear that Georgina was claiming right of way even though she was riding alone. She was making no attempt to move Beau over to let them pass.

'Whoa, Red,' called Bryony, bringing him to a halt. She heard her friends behind call to their ponies too and Josh's old bike squeak rustily to a stop at the back.

Although there was now space for Georgina to ride past, she halted Beau in the middle of the lane and looked Red up and down. Bryony immediately felt herself bristle. Georgina judged everyone, but especially her and Red.

Bryony's mind flicked back to the summer before last when she'd moved here from the city. Georgina Brook had owned Red then, but hadn't wanted him, or looked after him well. Georgina hated that now with Bryony as his owner, Red was doing beautifully.

'Oh, it's you lot,' said Georgina, confidently

stepping Beau forward. As she did, Red went to give him a friendly nuzzle but Georgina pulled Beau's head away.

'Don't go near him, Beau!' sniffed Georgina. 'He's so grubby!'

'It's just *sand*,' frowned Bryony. 'There's nothing wrong with a bit of sand.' She patted Red's neck. 'Red's been having fun with his friends.'

And at least, thought Bryony, she groomed Red herself. Whereas Georgina, who lived in the poshest house in town, got a few of the Brook Dale Manor staff to see to Beau.

Georgina raised her white-blonde eyebrows. Just like her pony, she was perfectly turned out. Her boots were polished, her riding jacket was crinkle-free, and there wasn't a single speck of mud – or sand – in sight.

Bryony became aware of her own clothes now. That morning she'd just grabbed the warmest things she could find, and it looked like her friends had too. Thick old fleeces, and mufflers and bobbly scarves, they were a muddle of mismatched layers. Bryony was also in her favourite hand-me-down jodhpurs.

'What's the hold-up?' asked Josh, now appearing at Red's side, but Georgina completely ignored this.

'I saw your mother this morning,' she said to Bryony.

'So?' Bryony shrugged back. The twins' mum was a florist, and had been busy doing the Manor's Christmas flower displays.

'She was working in my sitting room – in her big *muddy* cardigan,' Georgina continued with a shudder.

'*You* try being a florist and keeping clean!' cried Josh.

'No, thank you!' Georgina wrinkled up her nose. Then, raising her voice so the others could hear, 'Well!' she laughed. 'I hope she does a good job or I'll have to tell Daddy not to pay her!'

'Mrs May always does a *great* job!' called Alice.

'Yeah!' chorused Hari and Emma.

'Plus,' shouted Finn, 'no one knows more about flowers!'

Georgina smirked as if she couldn't care less, though Bryony thought she could detect a flash of annoyance in her eyes that the others had spoken up.

'Anyway,' said Georgina, 'I've got better things to do.' And tapping Beau's flanks, she trotted past them.

'Forget her,' muttered Josh as Bryony sighed.

'You're right,' nodded Bryony. She wouldn't let Georgina spoil the day.

They carried on down the lane, which gradually widened out so that now they could ride as a group. Red seemed back to his normal perky self after the encounter with Georgina had quietened him.

'But Piggy's definitely slowing,' said Emma. 'Which means he wants a snack.'

'We all want snacks at Christmas-time!' smiled Bryony.

She thought of the dreamy Christmas pastries on offer in the Lavender Lighthouse Tearoom, and the delicious shortbread stars iced with swirls. The holidays also meant no school for ages, so lots more time for hacks.

'Nowhere beats Brook Dale at Christmas!' grinned Bryony, and everyone agreed. It was pretty, and friendly, and there was so much to do!

'I like the carol singing best,' smiled Alice, 'in Market Square on Christmas Eve.'

'And buying presents!' said Hari.

'And wrapping them,' laughed Emma.

'And researching the history of Christmas,' nodded Finn. 'I found this brilliant book in the library.'

'Mince pies!' cried Josh. 'Tons of mince pies!'

'Well I,' said Bryony, 'love all the decorations. And so does Red!'

Seaview Stables was starting to look really Christmassy with a big silver star light now twinkling on the gate. And Abi, who was Bryony's favourite instructor, had told her there was more to come. Apparently the stable Christmas tree would have very special baubles this year too!

'Hey, Josh,' said Bryony, 'Gramps is coming round later to help us make our gingerbread house.'

'Cool!' smiled Josh. 'So no scoffing those jelly sweets . . .'

'As if!' Bryony grinned, patting her fleece pocket. Although she was tempted, these very special spiced cherry and apple flavour sweets made the perfect gingerbread-house roof tiles. They were coated in sugar that twinkled like frost, and smelled *delicious*.

They'd bought the sweets earlier from the post

office, and had been lucky to get them too. Miss Pigeon, who ran the place, only sold them at Christmas. And just to her favourite customers. Judging by the cherry smell on the old lady's breath, Bryony suspected she was squirrelling some away to secretly scoff herself!

'Em,' said Bryony quietly. 'Fancy helping with the gingerbread house?' Her mum had said she could invite someone and Emma was her best friend.

'Yes, please!' whispered Emma. 'Oh, but wait! I'm meant to be minding Will.'

Emma's parents were divorced and she sometimes helped out by looking after her little brother. 'Dad's got to get some rose bushes for the Brooks,' said Emma. Her dad was head gardener at Brook Dale Manor.

'That's okay,' said Bryony. 'Bring Will too. Mum won't mind.'

They stopped by the brook to let the ponies have a drink. As Bryony dismounted, Josh pedalled off to do a few wheelies down the lane.

'Mind the ice though,' Bryony called.

'No worries!'

Bryony watched Red drink the icy water as it bubbled over the stones. 'Oh, you're thirsty!' she said as he gently lapped it up.

Bryony looked around. It was such a pretty spot! The teasels were draped with spider webs, shimmering and winking with ice. The fence twinkled too. And the late-morning sun – lion-yellow in summer – today wore the colour of a soft ripe peach.

Bryony saw a robin on the drystone wall and Red then spotted it too. The bird started to chirp.

'He's singing "Jingle Bells",' cried Bryony and Red gave a happy little nicker.

'Ah!' laughed Bryony. 'And now *you're* joining in too!'

It was getting colder, but there was still no sign of snow. They jumped back on their ponies and veered off the lane down a pretty cross-country bridle path. As they went, Bryony blew into her scarf. She loved this scarf so much. It was big and soft and a gorgeous teal-blue. Dad had given it to her the Christmas before he'd died and it felt like a hug from him when she huddled it around her. It still *smelled* of Dad too. Just a little bit ...

The branches up above were dotted with balls of mistletoe which looked like giant baubles.

'Ooo!' cried Bryony. 'The Christmas Market's tomorrow! I wonder if Farmer Jenkins will be selling mistletoe?'

'He always does,' said Emma. 'And he's got tons at the farm.' Piggy lived in a field up at White Mouse Farm, so Emma had seen it.

Bryony's mum would have a stall at the Market too, selling door wreaths, flowerpots and winter posies. All of last week Mum had been busy making them. Plum Cottage had never looked so Christmassy!

As well as buying presents for her family at the Market, Bryony thought she might find something for her 'Friendship Jar'.

These Friendship Jars were another Brook Dale Christmas tradition. They were actually just jam jars with wire handles, labelled with a pretty tag. Each child in town made one for someone else, so that *everyone* would get a present and no one would be left out. In the jar you put a small thoughtful gift. Some home-made cookies maybe. Or all the bits for someone to make a tree decoration. It didn't have to be much. It was the thought that counted.

'Hey, Alice, who's your Friendship Jar person?' asked Bryony, but Hari shushed Alice immediately.

'*Bryony May!*' grinned Hari. '*That's meant to be a secret!*' Names were pulled from a hat, and you weren't supposed to say.

'If Alice *tells*, she'll turn into a toad!' nodded Josh. And puffing out their cheeks, everyone started to 'ribbit!' hysterically.

They were very nearly at Bluebell Wood now. Just one more bend to go. But as they approached it, Red stopped in his tracks, his head high and his ears forward.

'What is it, boy?' asked Bryony. Then she sniffed the air.

'Wood smoke!'

That was odd. Hardly anyone ever came out here as it was right on the outskirts of town.

'It's okay, Red,' said Bryony. 'Ah, but what's going on . . .?'

'Uh-oh,' laughed Josh. 'Ebony Swann's on the case!'

Ebony Swann was Bryony's TV detective hero.

Bryony never missed a single episode. And the more she watched, the more she longed for real–life mysteries to solve!

'It's probably just Farmer Jenkins,' said Emma. 'Burning snapped branches, I expect.'

'Yeah, tons came down in last night's storm,' Hari nodded.

'Well, there's only one way to find out,' beamed Bryony. 'Follow me!'

Chapter 2

Bryony trotted Red around the bend and there, set back in a small meadow on the outskirts of Bluebell Wood, was the prettiest little caravan she'd ever seen. 'It looks like it's out of a fairy tale, Red!' she smiled.

It was made out of wood, painted purplish-red, and decorated with flowers, fruit and birds.

At the front it had a little door in two parts which looked like a stable door, but smaller. Leading down from it was a fold-up ladder in the same pale yellow as the wooden wheels.

Arching over the top was a bright green domed roof with a chimney pipe to the left of the door. A ribbon of silver-grey smoke was trickling from it, dancing merrily up into the frosty sky.

Someone, thought Bryony, must be at home, and had lit their stove to keep warm. But the question was *who* could that someone be?

Her friends now appeared.

'Wow,' said Alice. 'And look behind the caravan too!'

Bryony stepped Red sideways so she could see. 'Oh, yes!'

Tied to one of the pines on the edge of the wood was a big strapping horse.

'It's a Shire,' said Finn. 'You can tell by its size and the feathering on its legs, see?' It was mainly black but its lower legs were white and fanned out like fringy tassels!

Bryony nodded. 'But it's so big.' She'd seen Shire horses in books before but didn't appreciate quite how huge they were.

'Easily about eighteen hands, I'd say,' said Hari.

To the left of the caravan was a smouldering campfire. Above it, dangling from a three-legged metal stand, was a huge black cast-iron kettle. A whisper of smoke curled up from the centre of the charred logs, the smell of which was pleasantly sweet.

'So that's why Red stopped back there,' said Bryony. 'He smelled the wood smoke.' She ruffled his mane. 'Clearly he's the Ebony Swann of the pony world!'

Bryony's gaze returned to the caravan. 'I wonder who lives inside?' she said.

'I guess whoever made those woodcarvings.' Josh pointed. 'See – there.'

Over by the fir trees at the entrance of the wood was the most enormous holly bush. In front of the bush, on the icy grass, sat a collection of little wooden animals.

'Oh!' gasped Bryony. They blended in so well!

There were fluffy-tailed squirrels, so realistic you'd think they'd just scampered from the trees. And there were rabbits and eagles and foxes and mice. There was *even* one big brown bear. At the bear's feet she noticed a painted sign ...

WOOD CARVINGS
FOR SALE

Then Bryony saw him, sitting on a tree stump, peering up at the snow clouds. A little wooden moon gazing hare. He was beautiful!

Bryony's dad, who'd been an artist, had once made a moon gazing hare out of clay. Dad had given it to Mum on her birthday, and Mum had called her Selena.

During the move to Brook Dale, though, Selena had got badly damaged. Bryony had been so sad for Mum, despite Mum putting on a very brave face about it.

Bryony had tried her best to mend Selena but there had been so many bits! In the end Selena was back in one piece, though not quite the same as before. Now one of her ears was decidedly wonky, and a foot was missing a chunk. But the worst thing was Selena's neck. It just wouldn't go back on right. So Selena could no longer gaze *up* at the moon as she sat on the window ledge at night. Now she had to gaze *down* at the lawn instead.

The moon gazing hare, thought Bryony, would make the perfect Christmas gift for Mum. And a wonderful new friend for Selena, too, who deserved one after everything she'd been through!

He could sit beside her on the window ledge each night and tell her how the moon winked and shone. And *she* could tell him about all the little animals that crept across the moonlit lawn. One looking up, and one looking down. Together they'd have the whole world covered . . .

Red, though, was still looking at the huge Shire horse.

'Like to go and say hello?' asked Bryony.

'But, Bry – that horse could squash Red flat!' Emma gasped.

Emma was still nervous around unfamiliar horses, though much better – thanks to Bryony – than she used to be.

'No, she looks friendly enough,' smiled Bryony. 'Don't worry.'

The huge Shire had now spotted Red too and was gazing back, calm and quiet. She had a pretty black face with a white stripe up the centre, which also went under her belly. Bryony thought she looked very steady and reliable.

Bryony dismounted. She would lead Red over

in case he got a bit twitchy. That way, she'd have better control, and it would be less threatening for the Shire too.

'Brr!' She stamped her feet. She could hardly feel them. It was getting chillier by the second. Holding Red's reins, she walked him across, while the others hung back to wait.

'Nice and steady, Red ...' Bryony whispered, keeping him close and making sure the Shire saw them coming.

She stopped a little way off from the horse, whose gaze hadn't left them.

'Hello there,' called Bryony and the Shire blinked back. Its big black ears moved forward to listen and its breathing was slow and relaxed.

'I'm Bryony and this is Red,' said Bryony. 'Pleased to meet you.'

She took a few steps closer with Red calmly at her side.

'That's the way,' said Bryony. Red was so dependable and Bryony was enormously proud of him. 'Good boy.'

They stopped by the horse, who bent to nuzzle Red's face, and Red replied with a whinny. Bryony knew that in the wild horses greeted each other by blowing on each other's noses and it looked like instinctively they were doing this now.

'You're lovely,' said Bryony, patting the horse's wide neck. Red looked like a little foal beside the Shire!

Bryony took two Polo mints out of her pocket. Red snaffled his off the palm of her hand, his whiskers tickly against her skin. Then the Shire horse licked the other mint up very gently.

Bryony smiled. 'So *you* like Polos too! But I wonder what your name is?'

'Blossom!' came a voice. Bryony spun around but there was nobody there. A giggle promptly followed from behind one of the trees, and out peeped a little girl. She looked about five or six – with freckles and a whirl of dark brown hair, quite as curly as Bryony's!

The girl skipped out and beamed up at Bryony. She was wearing a thick purple padded coat down to the knees of her jeans. On her feet were stripy wellies, and wrapped round and round her neck was a big orange scarf.

'But Blossom is a silly name!' giggled the girl.

She had a lisp as her top two baby teeth were missing, which also made her smile very cheeky. 'Because *I* think,' she went on, 'that Blossom is a *cow's* name, don't you?'

Bryony went to answer, but the girl snatched a breath then carried on chattering away ...

'So I call her Sparkle, because that's not a cow's name at all!'

'Oh, yes – good choice!' Bryony quickly chipped in as the girl did a twirl on the grass. 'Yes, she definitely looks like a Sparkle to me!' laughed Bryony.

The girl carried on twirling until she fell down dizzy. But jumping straight back up, she grinned.

'I'm Meredith Cooper. But I *wish* I was called Alice – like that girl in *Alice in Wonderland*. Mummy's reading me the book, and Alice is my favourite. And the White Rabbit is too. I love rabbits. And doing ballet twirls! What's your name?'

Before Bryony could reply, the girl started a fresh twirl.

'I'm Bryony,' smiled Bryony. 'Bryony May. And this is Red. Oh, and those people over there are my friends. One's even called Alice – just like the Alice in your book!'

Meredith stopped twirling, looked across to the others, then back at Red beside Blossom.

'Red's so tiny he'd fit in a *teapot*,' giggled Meredith. 'I don't think he'd be able to pull our caravan, do you?'

'He'd certainly try!' Bryony grinned back. 'But I guess you're probably right. Red jumps like a dream, though. He's the gymkhana jumping champ! So *you* live in that caravan then, do you?'

Meredith nodded back. 'With my mum and dad and brother.'

'Do you know how much that moon gazing hare costs?' asked Bryony. 'The one on the tree stump. He's so sweet! I'd really love to buy him as a Christmas present for my mum.'

'He's called Hector,' replied Meredith. 'We're selling him at the Market, but I don't know how much he costs.'

Looking back across to the lane, Meredith then whispered, 'Don't tell your friends, but *your* pony's the cutest.'

'Thanks, Meredith!' Bryony smiled.

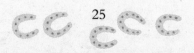

Just then, a small boy came running from the woods. He had the same dark curly hair as Meredith, but was slightly taller and plumper.

'Oi, Meredith!' he panted. He looked very cross. 'You're not supposed to talk to strangers!'

'I'm not!' frowned Meredith, her freckly nose in the air. 'This is Bryony – and Red!'

Meredith turned to Bryony. 'Me and Morgan are twins – but *I'm* the oldest,' she announced.

'Snap!' beamed Bryony. 'I'm an oldest twin too.'

'Don't mean you're the *best* though,' Morgan nodded. His big brown eyes, much lighter than his sister's, looked determined.

With that the caravan door opened and a lady's head peeped out. 'Meredith, Morgan – lunch,' she called brightly. 'Come, come!'

Then she saw Bryony standing by the twins and her smile faded at once.

'I *told* her not to talk to strangers, Mum!' said Morgan. He looked at his sister who shuffled guiltily.

'Sorry!' gasped Bryony. 'I-It was my fault. I came over.' The last thing she wanted was Meredith to be in trouble because of *her*.

'See, I was just passing,' Bryony went on, 'and wanted to say hello to your horse. We're like that in Brook Dale. Not nosy! Just . . . friendly, so . . .'

Bryony's voice trailed off and in the corner of her eye she saw her friends start to backtrack up the lane, probably sensing it was for the best.

The twins' mum had opened the caravan door and was standing at the top of the steps. Her skin was very fair and her hair dark and wavy. It was swept off her face with a flowery headscarf tied into a softly hanging bow. She was wearing a thick green jumper and an ankle-length skirt – charcoal grey, made out of heavy wool.

'We just travel a lot,' Mrs Cooper said. Her voice was soft but tinged with apprehension. 'And people can be friendly, or . . . well . . . not so much.'

'Yes,' replied Bryony. 'Yes, I understand.'

Mrs Cooper nodded back with a faint smile. But while Morgan read nothing into this smile and began to head to the caravan, Meredith must have taken it to mean that her mother was now fine with Bryony – as Bryony then felt a tiny hand wriggle into hers.

'Can Bryony read to me, Mum?' asked Meredith.

'Not now, sweetheart,' Mrs Cooper replied gently. 'It's lunchtime.'

Morgan squeezed in past his mum.

'Tomorrow then?' asked Meredith. 'After the Christmas Market? Please ... she wants to be my friend.'

Bryony waited to see what Mrs Cooper would say. She hoped she would agree. Meredith reminded Bryony so much of herself when she'd been younger – and even now. Busy and chatty and friendly. And *very* determined!

Making friends, she imagined, must be hard if you're always travelling from place to place. When Bryony had first come to Brook Dale she'd longed for friends too ...

'She doesn't give up, does she?' said Mrs Cooper, and Bryony shook her head with a grin.

'I, um ... could come after the Market,' said Bryony. 'If it's okay with you and my mum.'

Mrs Cooper looked thoughtful.

'Ask your mother,' she said finally. 'And then, well ... we'll see.'

'Hooray!' cheered Meredith. She gave Bryony a huge hug before running inside for her lunch.

'Thanks, Mrs Cooper,' Bryony called up. 'And I'm sure at the Market you'll see for yourself what a friendly place Brook Dale is!'

Then, quickly mounting Red, she trotted off to find the others. Time to go and make that gingerbread house!

Chapter 3

Back at Seaview, Bryony wasted no time in giving Red a thorough brush down to remove any caked-on sand and mud.

'Back in your cosy stable!' she said and Red replied with a happy but sleepy-sounding whinny. He seemed really content living at Seaview, and why wouldn't he be? It was busy, and friendly, with pony pals absolutely everywhere!

Bryony felt lucky he could live here too. Stabling a pony was very expensive and when Grandpa had bought Red, although it felt like a dream, Bryony had also been a bit worried about how they'd afford to keep him.

They were managing, though. Just about. And

Bryony tried her best to help. She happily chipped in practically all of her pocket money, and was always thinking up ways to make more.

She also fed, exercised and mucked out Red herself, which helped no end with costs. But actually she wouldn't have had it any other way. The more time she spent with him the better!

Finally, as part of his half livery deal, Red gave other riders lessons from time to time. Again though, Bryony was fine with this. No one could love Red as much as she did. And clearly she was *his* favourite too!

'Smart boy!' said Bryony when Red's coat was soft and shiny. She popped his brushes and combs back in her carry bag. Then, topping up his hay net and water bucket, she hugged him and left him in peace to have his nap.

Out in the yard the sky was dark grey and the clouds looked even higher than before. Bryony rubbed her hands together excitedly. 'Let it snow, let it snow, *let it snow*!'

She ran all the way home, ready for lunch. Then she'd make that gingerbread house. She was really looking forward to Grandpa coming!

'Hi!' panted Bryony, rushing in through the door.

'Come inside from the cold,' called Mum. The kitchen looked so pretty, lit with lamps and fairy lights. And on every spare surface, in buckets, jugs and jars, were hand-tied posies to sell at tomorrow's Christmas Market.

'What's for lunch?' asked Bryony.

'Parsnip soup,' replied Mum as she stood by the Aga stirring it.

'Smells ready to me,' Josh called from the table, spoon in hand.

Bryony hung up her fleece and scarf, washed her hands at the sink, then hurried to join her brother.

'Here we are,' said Mum, bringing over the soup and setting down the bowls between yet more festive posies.

'Don't get me wrong, I like flowers,' said Josh. 'But it feels like we're eating in a jungle!'

Bryony laughed as she dipped her bread into the soup. She blew on it and wolfed it down.

'Mmm . . .' she said. It tasted delicious. Just what she needed after that freezing-cold hack!

'I wonder what Meredith and Morgan will be having?' Bryony said to Josh.

'Who?' asked Mum.

'They're twins!' replied Bryony. 'Passing through Brook Dale with their mum and dad.' And she and Josh told Mum about earlier on.

'So their caravan,' said Josh, 'is really cool. And their parents make these brilliant wooden—'

'Josh!' shrieked Bryony. She kicked him under the table before he went and blurted out about the sculptures.

'Ow!' said Josh. 'What did you kick me for?'

'Oh, sorry,' said Bryony. 'I . . . jerky legs! Could you pass some bread over, please?'

'Err, the bread's right in front of you.' Josh looked puzzled. But then the penny must have dropped, for Josh gave a big wink back.

'Why are you winking, Josh?' asked Mum.

'Um – fly in my eye!' Josh gulped.

Mum raised her eyebrows. 'If I didn't know better, I'd guess you two were up to something.'

'Us?' Josh grinned.

'As if!' blushed Bryony. 'Anyway, Mum, as Josh was saying, the twins' caravan is really pretty. And the little girl – Meredith – she's so sweet and chatty! I promised I'd go and see her after the Christmas Market tomorrow, if that's okay with you?'

'Um . . .' Mum looked a little unsure.

'Just to read her a quick story,' Bryony added. 'I think she *so* wants to be friends. I really liked her, and Red liked Blossom – and he's a very good judge of character.'

'Well . . . all right then,' said Mum. 'I'll give you a lift across.'

'Oh, thanks, Mum!'

They finished their soup and had a clementine each, still chatting about the Coopers.

'Hmm, now I come to think of it,' said Mum. 'I might have seen Meredith's dad over at Brook Dale Manor this morning.'

'How come?' asked Bryony.

'Collecting branches,' Mum replied. 'Lots came down in the storm last night and I think he might have been helping Emma's dad to tidy up.'

Emma's dad was probably glad of the help too, thought Bryony. The Brooks always worked him flat out!

'But how do you know it was Meredith's dad when you've never seen him before?' asked Bryony.

'Good question!' said Mum. 'Well, I just figured that everyone knows everyone in Brook Dale. But I didn't know the man at the Brooks's. So when you just said the Coopers were passing through I put two and two together. He came asking Mrs Brook if he could help pick up sticks in exchange for some bundles of branches.'

'It probably was him then because they do have a stove. I saw a pipe chimney on their caravan,' said Bryony.

'*Plus*, he'd need sticks for their campfire,' added Josh. He turned back to Mum. 'Great detective work!'

'Yes, watch out, Ebony Swann, I say!' laughed Bryony.

When they'd finished their fruit, Mum brought over a tin.

'Yesss!' cried the twins. It was a special selection biscuit tin she only ever bought at Christmas. Bryony's eyes lit up when Mum took off the lid.

'It *really* feels like Christmas now!' she cried.

She insisted that Mum had first pick, and was most relieved when she took the coffee crunch. Josh went next and, as usual, chose the jammy ring. Bryony then made a beeline for the chocolate orange wrapped in shiny foil.

She squirrelled it across to the rocking chair by the Aga, the most snuggly spot in the cottage. On her way over, she glanced through the window. Still no snow but those clouds were big and puffy!

'*You* don't want snow though, do you?' she said to Blueberry Muffin, curled up on the rocking chair.

The fat grey cat ignored her, pretending to be asleep. He'd been hogging the best chair for weeks! Since the weather had turned frosty he'd hardly gone out, except when he'd been desperate for the loo. Then he'd stomp back in looking furiously frozen, his tail fluffed out like a toilet brush!

'*I* think you need the loo *now*,' giggled Bryony, kneeling by the chair in front of Berry. The cat's ears gave a twitch but his eyes stayed firmly shut. Bryony sighed. He wasn't going anywhere.

'Right then,' she said. And, deciding to be brave, she scooped him up gently, sat down on the chair and placed him back down on her lap.

The tip of his tail twitched warningly but his claws, for the moment, didn't appear.

'There!' said Bryony. Berry weighed a ton,

but was very warm and fluffy. And as she ate her biscuit, Bryony toasted her toes by the Aga.

'Have you had a good morning then, Mum?' she asked.

'Yes!' replied Mum. 'Very busy, you know, but I managed to finish all the Manor's mantelpiece decorations. Tomorrow it's the bannister, then I'm done. It *was* a bit hectic over there, though. The plumbers were back in fixing some drain problems, and things were a bit tense with Georgina.'

'Tense?' repeated Bryony. She sat up in her chair. 'Was Georgina mean to you?' she asked, remembering Georgina's earlier comment about Mum's cardigan.

'She'd better not have been nasty.' Josh frowned just as Grandpa came in.

'Who?'

'Who's always nasty to *everyone*?' tutted Josh.

'Georgina Brook?' suggested Grandpa, needing no time to think, and Bryony and Josh both nodded.

'Anyway, no,' continued Mum. 'She wasn't nasty to *me*. Her mother was in the firing line today. Georgina's school, I think, are going on some ski trip but her parents have said she can't go.'

'Why?' asked Josh.

'Because her great-aunt is coming for the holidays,' replied Mum. 'And would really like to see her.'

Bryony raised her eyebrows, completely baffled as to why *anyone* would want to see Georgina.

'So, what happened next?' Grandpa grabbed a custard cream. 'After they said no to the ski trip?'

'Well, from what I could gather,' said Mum, 'the morning after they said she couldn't go, Mrs Brook went out to the garden, and all the winter roses – every single one – had mysteriously lost their heads in the night!'

'That's no *mystery*!' Bryony cried. '*That* was clearly *Georgina*!'

Mum nodded. 'Right. But she's saying it was an "accident" when she was trying to "snip off the straggly bits"!'

'It was her temper more like,' Grandpa nodded.

'So today,' said Mum, 'as her dad's away on business, she was targeting her mother, who usually gives in. But Mrs Brook wasn't having it! So Georgina was horrid.'

'Wow,' gasped Bryony. 'Beheading prize roses is

bad – even for *her*! Emma said her dad was buying new roses. Now we know why. Yikes!'

'She's blown the ski trip then!' shrugged Josh. But Bryony wasn't so sure. Georgina usually got her own way in the end.

It was time to clear up after lunch. While Mum washed the soup bowls and Grandpa dried, Bryony and Josh found the ingredients to make the gingerbread house. They were just laying them out on the table when Emma and Will arrived, wrapped up like Arctic explorers!

'I'm sure it's going to snow any second,' said Emma, pulling off her coat and big bobble hat.

'Oooh!' cried Bryony, crossing her fingers. 'I hope so!'

Emma thanked Bryony's mum for having them round. Then, turning to her little brother, she whispered, 'Give her the gift then. You remember what they are, right?'

'Yep!' Will nodded. And stepping forward, he held out a pretty painted flowerpot with some shoots poking out of the soil.

'Sprout flowers!' said Will. 'Happy Christmas from us!'

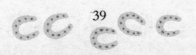

'Not *sprout* flowers, Will!' Emma looked horrified. 'Dad said they are *sprouting*, not *sprouts*!'

'Crocuses?' asked Mum, and Emma nodded back.

'Yellow, purple and white ones.'

'Oh, lovely!' Mum took them. 'And so kind of you too! Please say thanks to your dad.'

'Now can we make that gingerbread house?' asked Will.

Mum nodded. 'Of course! And Grandpa will help.'

Then, armed with some scissors and a big bundle of string, she headed to the lounge to do something she called 'top secret'.

'Wrapping!' whispered Josh.

'Presents!' gasped Bryony excitedly.

And the excitement just went on and on. Baking the gingerbread house was great. As they weighed and stirred, they sang Christmas songs and kept 'testing' the mixture with their fingers. When questioned by Grandpa, Josh called this the dip-and-lick method!

When all the baked house bits came out of the Aga, they looked, and smelled, really good. Grandpa placed them on a wire rack to cool while the children made some animals from the leftover dough. They had a pony, a pig, a cat, a dog, and a Tyrannosaurus rex. The plan was for the little farmyard pals (and Josh's killer dinosaur!) to stand in the garden of the gingerbread house looking festive.

'Right,' said Bryony when the house bits were cool. 'Time to glue it together.'

'But won't glue stick our *teeth* together too?' asked Will.

'Not *glue* glue, Will!' snorted Josh. 'We use, um . . . something else.'

'Royal icing,' said Bryony.

'Yeah,' nodded Josh. 'I was just about to say that!'

Bryony mixed some up. Then they each filled an icing bag and piped up the side of the walls. They joined the sides together as they went, Grandpa trying his best to hold them in place until the icing set.

The roof went on next. Then the chimney pot. It made Bryony think of the little pipe chimney which poked up out of Meredith's caravan. It looked so cheerful. So friendly!

Then suddenly Bryony had a worrying thought.

She'd told Mrs Cooper that Brook Dale was friendly, but what with beheaded flowers, and strops, and icy stares – it didn't *feel* that welcoming right now.

But the Brooks weren't the only family here, she thought. Other people would surely welcome the Coopers and their adorable menagerie of little wooden animals. Wouldn't they . . .?

'I love piping!' cried Will, and Bryony's attention swiftly returned to the gingerbread house. They piped on a door and windows, then rows of little loops for roof tiles. Into the centre of each loop they did a dot of icing then stuck on the special Christmas jelly sweets. The sugar twinkled like frost and the smell of spiced apple and cherry filled the air.

'Mmm . . .' said everyone. It was glorious!

They finished the house with some icicles hanging down. Then Josh went and found some old toy fences which they iced into place around the tray it was on.

Will arranged their biscuit animals in a friendly cluster, finally wedging the T. rex in the chimney pot.

'So he won't eat the others,' Will explained. 'Because that's not friendly at Christmas.'

And then, as they showed their house off to Mum, Bryony gave a squeal and pointed to the window.

'It's snowing!'

Chapter 4

Forgetting all about hats and scarves, the children raced outside to see the snow. Little flakes were tumbling out of the sky, twirling like dainty ballerinas.

'Wheee!' Bryony started to twirl too, round and round, just like Meredith. 'At last!' she cried. Snow made everything magical!

'I really hope it'll stick,' said Josh.

'If it does,' said Emma, 'tomorrow we could make a snowman.'

'Or a snow *pony*?' Bryony suggested.

'I'll help!' cried Will.

'*And*,' grinned Josh, 'we can all have a snowball fight!'

But they had to wait for enough snow to do that. For now, they dashed about catching the snowflakes, or spun around, their faces to the sky, until they fell down dizzy in fits of laughter.

Soon the snow started to ice Plum Cottage so it looked just like their gingerbread house! Then Grandpa appeared, carrying a tray.

'Hot chocolate!' he called.

'Hooray!' everyone cheered, and they huddled on the bench beside the shed to drink it.

As Bryony swallowed the last glorious mouthful, she noticed it was starting to get dark. She checked her watch. It was almost five o'clock.

'I have to go,' she said. 'Red needs his supper.'

'Oh, and Piggy!' Emma cried.

'Come on then,' said Bryony. 'Before it's pitch black.' Emma had to trek all the way to White Mouse Farm, up the steepest hill in Brook Dale.

'You stay here, Will,' Emma told her brother. 'Dad's coming to fetch you later.'

'Okay!' Will looked delighted to be staying with Josh. He loved Josh's technical Lego and his comics.

The girls nipped inside to say they were off,

then walked together as far as Seaview. It was still snowing, but only very lightly.

They stopped by the big four-bar gate leading into the stables. 'See you in the morning,' Bryony said. Emma was heading straight home after seeing Piggy.

'Meet here at eight?' Emma asked, tiny snowflakes clinging to her hair.

'Sounds good to me,' Bryony nodded. Tomorrow was going to be a very busy day so best start it nice and early.

With a wave, Emma carried on up Lighthouse Lane and Bryony opened the gate. Coming down the path from the main stable block was Lavender Jones, the kind old lady who ran the tearoom in the Stormy Point Lighthouse. She often delivered cakes and sandwiches to the Seaview staff.

Bryony held open the gate for her.

'Oh, thank you, Bryony,' Lavender said. 'How are you, my dear?'

'Very well, thanks. How are you?' asked Bryony.

Lavender smiled. 'Really busy today but that's how I like it! I've just brought Abi a batch of my Christmas cupcakes.'

'Ooo! I love those!' Bryony smiled. They came in chocolate and vanilla flavours and Lavender iced ponies and dainty little snowflakes on top.

'I wish I could bake like you,' said Bryony.

'I'll teach you,' Lavender replied.

Bryony's eyes lit up at once. 'Oh, thank you! When can we start?'

'January?'

'Brilliant!' Bryony cried. Something to look forward to after all the fun of Christmas!

Bryony was really fond of Lavender. Last spring Bryony had solved a very tricky mystery which meant Lavender could stay in Brook Dale for good – *and* get back the old lighthouse, which was once her family home.

Lavender had been so grateful for this that she now kept the room at the top of the lighthouse just for Bryony and her friends. It was circular with windows all around, and because the lighthouse jutted into the sea, being in it made you feel like you were right in the middle of the ocean.

The Super Six had named it 'Lookout Towers' and it had become their HQ. Every Wednesday after school they met there to play games, or in the absence of *real-life* mysteries to solve, to write their own Whodunnits. Bryony had also set up a Cluedo tournament, which currently she was winning!

'See you on Wednesday then,' Lavender nodded. 'Any new mysteries to solve?'

Bryony shook her head. 'Sadly not, so we might make our Friendship Jars instead.' It was only four days until Christmas Eve, which was when the postman delivered them.

'Oh!' said Bryony. She'd just had a thought. 'I might do *two* jars this year!'

She'd drawn Cabbage Patch Charlie from the hat, who had lived by himself since his wife had died. But why not do a jar for Meredith's family too? To help welcome them to Brook Dale for Christmas, since this was the place they'd chosen to spend their holidays.

'Good for you!' said Lavender. 'But no saying who they're for, or . . .'

'. . . I'll turn into a toad!' Bryony giggled. 'I know!'

With a laugh, Lavender set off through the snow, and Bryony headed in through the gate.

The fence and gate had fairy lights on now. Abi

must have hung them up that afternoon. This was all getting more and more festive and exciting!

Bryony hurried up the path and round into the yard, where she almost bumped into Abi who was up a stepladder, looping lights around the office door.

'They're lovely!' Bryony called up to her.

'Thanks, Bry,' Abi smiled back. 'I was meaning to do it all of last week, and I finally pick the day it snows. Red's out in the field. He hasn't been out long as he's just done a lesson but he can probably come in now.'

'I'll fetch him,' Bryony said.

The yard was busy as riders came and went. People were pushing wheelbarrows, cleaning tack and mucking out. And a boy called Arthur Dobbs, who wore long shorts in all weathers, was red-faced and puffing as he brushed the snowy yard.

Bryony waited as a group led their ponies past, bringing them in from the paddock and field.

'Hey, Bry!' said a girl with a glossy chestnut mare.

'Oh, hi, Jess,' replied Bryony. 'Destiny okay?'

'Yeah, she's *loving* the snow!' Jess patted her pony. 'Time for supper now though.'

'I'm just getting Red in too,' said Bryony. 'See you!'

She headed off to the field, where Red was playfully snorting into the snow.

'Having fun?' laughed Bryony. She patted his side and he turned and nuzzled her arm. She loved how he was always so pleased to see her!

'Ahhh ...' She stroked the white star between his eyes as his kiss curl twinkled with snowflakes.

'I wish I had a camera, Red,' Bryony said. 'This would make a gorgeous Christmas card!'

When Bryony had first met Red his big brown eyes had looked sad. Not any more! Now they were shining with happiness!

'Come on, then,' she said. 'Let's get you inside and we'll play in the snow tomorrow.' She clipped on his lead rein and led him out of the field, her boots squeaking in the freshly fallen snow.

Back in the yard Finn wobbled past with a wheelbarrow piled high with dirty straw.

'Mind the floor, Bry. It's really slippery,' he said.

'Huh! It shouldn't be!' puffed Arthur, still sweeping. 'I'm on it, don't you worry. And the mounting block is spotless – look!'

He pointed across the yard. Arthur loved cleaning – even though he'd swear blind he didn't.

'You're doing a great job,' Bryony called, and Arthur beamed.

'But it's a horrible job,' he added as an afterthought. 'Really grim!'

Finn and Bryony exchanged grins, then Bryony led Red into his stable. 'Now let's check your hooves and brush you down,' she said.

Bryony always started with his front hooves and followed the same routine so Red knew what was coming.

Placing her hand near his shoulder, she ran it down his side and then down the back of his leg. When she got to the fetlock, she asked Red for his hoof, and when he lifted it, Bryony held it nice and relaxed.

'Well done, Red!' she said. He was very good at giving her his hooves now.

As Red was now balanced on three legs, Bryony needed to work carefully but quickly. With the hoof pick, she flicked out the mud around his frog, working from the back to the front. She did the same around the front of his shoe, finishing off with a quick brush all over.

Red was standing really well, and Bryony praised him lots. She repeated this with the other three hooves. Although she only found mud in them today, if it carried on snowing then tomorrow, she knew, trapped snow and balls of ice might be a problem.

She quickly checked her Pony Handbook. There might be something she could rub in, hopefully to stop that happening. 'Ah! Vaseline mixed with cooking oil,' read Bryony. She was pretty sure she had both these things at home.

Next she brushed Red, and as she did, she told him all about the Friendship Jar she'd just decided to give the Coopers.

'I hope they'll like it,' Bryony said. Meredith especially *so* wanted to be her friend. And she was so sweet and funny.

'And tomorrow, Red,' said Bryony, 'if the snow sticks, we're going to build a snow *pony*.'

Red listened, blowing gently and standing patiently until his coat was as shiny as a toffee apple. 'But *no* snow pony,' smiled Bryony, 'would *ever* look as handsome as you!'

After Bryony had seen to Red's supper she

banked up the stable with lots of extra straw to keep him snug overnight. Then popping out to the tack room, she quickly returned with his blanket. In one of the corners was his name, which Lavender had kindly embroidered. It was super-warm too, which was just as well. The thermometer on the yard wall already said below freezing and it was only going to get colder overnight.

It was almost time for Seaview to close so, popping on Red's blanket, Bryony hugged him goodnight and headed across to the door. But instead of leaving, she turned and just watched him for a moment.

'I'm the luckiest girl in the world to have you,' she said as Red nibbled his hay. He stopped and whinnied, as if to say ...

'And I'm luckiest pony in the world to have you!'

A beaming Bryony now stepped outside and closed the door behind her. It was dark and still snowing but lots of stars were out and the moon shone like silver.

She was just about to head off home when who should she see across the yard but Georgina Brook.

Georgina was talking to a girl called Amber Stepney, who was bringing her pony, Dash, back in.

'Hmmm,' said Bryony.

This was very odd.

Georgina hardly ever came to Seaview because Beau had a state-of-the-art stable at the Manor. And when she *did* come, she only had time for her posh school friends. Amber Stepney wasn't one of those. So why was Georgina here? And what could she want with Amber?

Bryony watched.

Georgina and Amber appeared to be arguing. Georgina looked really cross about something and Amber kept nervously playing with her long bright ginger hair.

Bryony began to quietly edge across the yard, desperate to hear what they were saying. The longer they didn't see her, the more she'd find out. Already she could feel her heart start to quicken at the thought of a mystery in the making. But any mystery involving Georgina Brook usually spelled trouble!

When she got close enough to hear, Bryony

paused and hung back. She was right – Georgina and Amber *were* in mid-argument . . .

'He was meant to come back!' Bryony heard Georgina snap. 'So where could he be *now*?'

'How should *I* know?' replied Amber. 'I haven't seen him all day. But he doesn't always listen – I do know that. And he gets muddled all the time. Why do you want him anyway?'

'It's none of your business! Just tell him from—'

But Georgina stopped mid-flow, having just spotted Bryony.

'Stop *earwigging*!' scowled Georgina.

'I wasn't!' blushed Bryony, knowing full well she *was*. 'I was just . . . walking to the gate.'

'Well then!' snapped Georgina. 'What are you waiting for? Walk!'

Bryony carried on past them, her head in a whirl. There was definitely something fishy going on.

Who was the *he*, Georgina was on about? Why was he meant to come back? And from where?

Bryony knew she wouldn't rest until she got some answers.

'Curiouser and curiouser . . .' she said to herself, like Meredith's Alice in Wonderland.

And Brook Dale was starting to *look* like Wonderland too as Bryony set off home, deep in thought – and *snow*.

'A Winter Wonderland Mystery!' she grinned. 'What could be more perfect?'

Chapter 5

The ponies were giddy with excitement when they were turned out into the Seaview paddock early on Tuesday morning. The snow had stuck. It was beautiful. 'And it's *still* snowing!' Bryony cried.

'Told you,' said Finn.

'Yep,' nodded Bryony. This was going to be a brilliant day!

Emma pointed out Red trotting about, his tail high and his ears forward.

'It looks like he's *dancing*,' Bryony laughed. He was lifting his front legs up very high as if doing a Spanish trot!

Daffy, however, looked much less graceful as she

rolled on the snow-covered grass. It was like she had a big itch that needed scratching!

Even Tornado – not a fan of sudden changes – wasn't fazed by the snow at all. He was batting the falling snowflakes with his nose, as if trying to work them out.

'So, I was reading him an article, just last week,' said Finn, 'entitled "Cracking the Code on Snow Crystals".'

'Ah,' grinned Hari. 'I expect he's testing out the theory then!'

Princess Perla then broke into a gallop, ready for a bit of action.

'Wow, Alice – she's a Princess warrior!' cried Bryony and Alice gave a gasp.

'I knew she was fast, but look at her go. Eeek!'

Snow was flying off the elegant palomino's back hooves as she tore around the paddock.

'Princess P was born to pull a chariot!' cried Josh.

'And now she has *troops*,' Emma laughed.

All the other ponies were galloping off after her. Except Piggy, of course, who was trying to *eat* the snowflakes.

Leaving them to it, the Super Six hurried off to

have some snowy fun of their own. Hari led the way to the field near the lighthouse. It was very close to the paddock so they could easily nip back to check the ponies.

'Oh, wow!' cried Bryony when they arrived. The field was completely covered in snow, which, apart from a smattering of foxy footprints, was smooth. And being so close to the headland meant you could see for miles.

Bryony looked at the view. It was stunning! The surrounding hills were dazzlingly white, like they'd been iced for Christmas. The beach was snowy too – and so were the caves. They looked like Santa's grotto!

'Beautiful, right?' Alice beamed as Bryony's friends now gathered around.

Bryony nodded. 'Christmas has come at last!'

She hoped the Coopers liked it too. Of all the places they might have gone at this special time, they had chosen to travel here. Brook Dale just *had* to deliver them a magical Christmas!

She thought of their little caravan. It probably looked gorgeous dusted in snow. She imagined the family inside it, toasty warm, a thin ribbon of smoke from their chimney curling into the snowflakes.

Bryony couldn't wait to see Meredith later. Being a good friend was important to her. It was also something she'd always done well. Plus, by the time the Christmas Market was done, Meredith's parents would have seen for themselves that Brook Dale cared for *everyone* – locals and visitors. Their gorgeous woodcarvings would probably sell like hot cakes!

But first things first. Bryony had promised Josh a snowball fight. So, when no one was looking, she balled up some snow, took aim and sent it flying.

Smack!

It exploded all over Josh's bobble hat.

'Bullseye!' laughed Bryony as her brother spun around.

'Right then!' he grinned. 'This means *war.*'

With a shriek, Bryony fled to a big bank of trees, Emma and Alice behind her.

'Oh, but Josh has got Finn – and *Hari*,' groaned Alice. Hari was super-competitive.

'Never mind!' cried Bryony. 'Up this tree, guys – quick!'

The girls scrambled up a huge sturdy oak tree with lots of big, low-lying branches. Seconds later the enemy advanced, flinging snowballs left, right and centre.

'Ow!' A whizzer got Bryony on the nose. But Alice and Emma were scooping snow off the branches and raining down snowy cannonballs too.

'You'll never win, Josh!' cried Bryony, forgetting Hari was a gymnast. As Josh and Finn batted the girls' snowballs away, Hari was up the tree like a shot.

'And guess what?' grinned Hari, reaching Bryony in seconds. Hari whipped a secret snowball out of the hood of her coat and stuffed it down the neck of Bryony's jacket.

'It's freeeeeeezing!' Bryony was howling with laughter.

'I've taken your castle!' Hari declared. 'We win!'

Still in hysterics, the girls climbed out of the tree and Josh's army swiftly took them prisoners.

'And the losers,' announced Hari, 'clean all the ponies' tack!'

'Ooo, I like cleaning tack!' smiled Alice and the others all laughed – 'Trust you!'

Just then, Emma's dad appeared with Will. Mr Lawrence was wearing a scarf with little robins on and his usual threadbare olive jacket. And Will was in a duffle coat and a hat that looked like a reindeer!

'We thought you might be peckish,' said Mr Lawrence.

'So we brought you these,' said Will. He held out two nets of chocolate coins wrapped in gold foil.

This was just what they needed after all that running. They sat on a tree stump and tucked in. Emma's dad and Will sat with them too. Mr Lawrence said he was really pleased for the break as it made a nice change from planting rose bushes!

'Especially as it was unnecessary,' said Bryony. 'Georgina chopping the roses' heads off was ridiculous.'

'What?!' cried Hari. So Bryony and Josh filled her in.

Everyone was shocked that even Georgina would spoil such lovely roses.

'But, Mr Lawrence,' said Finn, 'isn't the ground too cold for new roses to be planted right now?'

Mr Lawrence looked impressed.

'I read a book on it once,' added Finn.

'Ah, I see,' said Mr Lawrence. 'And yes, Finn, you're quite right.'

'So why plant them,' said Alice, 'if there's a good chance they won't survive?'

'Because,' sighed Mr Lawrence, 'when the Brooks say they want bushes with actual roses on *now*, there's really no point arguing.'

Bryony sat up at the mention of the word 'arguing', recalling Georgina's argument with Amber Stepney last night at Seaview.

She'd mentioned it to Josh, but the morning's snow had taken over and she hadn't yet told the others. Bryony knew, though, that the argument would bang about in her brain until she got some answers.

'Mr Lawrence,' said Bryony, 'is Georgina still grumpy? Mum said she was fuming yesterday.'

'Hmm, I'm afraid so,' Mr Lawrence replied. 'I really shouldn't gossip, I suppose, but Mr Brook came home earlier from a few days' business. Will and I were in the garden planting and we saw him go inside. Anyway, soon after, we could hear Georgina yelling.'

'About what?' asked Bryony.

'Well, her Great-aunt Agatha is coming, I think, and making her miss out on ...'

'... skiing?' chipped in Bryony, and Mr Lawrence nodded.

'Quite so.'

'So what did Mr Brook say to that?' asked Josh.

'Actually, nothing,' Mr Lawrence replied. 'Because suddenly *he* started yelling too about something that had gone missing.'

'What?' asked Bryony.

'We dunno,' frowned Will. ''Cos then Dad moved us saying we shouldn't be listening!'

'And Dad was quite right,' Mr Lawrence replied. 'So yes, Georgina is still very cross. But I suppose it could be worse.'

'How?' asked Bryony.

'Well,' said Mr Lawrence, 'at least the Manor's toilets are finally back in action as the plumbers finished yesterday afternoon.'

'Huh! I'd *love* to have seen Georgina without a loo,' snorted Hari. And she put on her posh Georgina voice: '*I shall only use a chamber pot if it's finest bone china!*'

Bryony and her friends burst out laughing and even Mr Lawrence couldn't hold in a chuckle. Bryony imagined Georgina holding a potty – and her nose – hilarious!

'Right then,' said Mr Lawrence. 'I'd best get back.' And leaving Will with Emma, he headed off.

'And, guys, I have news,' Bryony said, and she told the others about Georgina's Seaview visit.

'But what could she want there?' Alice looked puzzled. '*Our* stables aren't usually good enough.'

'Exactly!' cried Bryony in the tone of Ebony Swann. 'So something's up for sure! Plus, she was *arguing* with Amber Stepney so I think *that's* important too.'

'Arguing about what?' Finn quickly asked.

'I'm not sure,' Bryony replied. 'Georgina was on about some "he" or other – who should have "come right back". But Amber knew nothing and said she hadn't even seen him.'

'*Amber Stepney* . . .' repeated Hari. 'Hang on a sec, isn't her sister in our form at school?'

'Oh, yes!' cried Bryony. 'Her sister's Jasmine.'

'But they don't live here,' Emma said. 'They come in on the school bus.'

Bryony shrugged. 'I don't know much about them. Or what Georgina would want with Amber. I do sit with Jasmine in History but we've only really talked about Henry the Eighth – oh, and coalmining.'

She thought for a moment. 'Anyway,' said Bryony, 'we *definitely* have a mystery-in-the-making here so let's carry on the investigation at Lookout Towers tomorrow at five.'

'The Super Six are on the case again!' grinned Josh. 'Tell Lavender mine's a chocolate milkshake.'

'I think, by now, she probably knows that!' laughed Alice.

While the friends had been chatting, Will had made a snow pony. It looked like a funny-shaped potato with a wonky stick tail but he'd really tried his best.

'What do you think?' he asked the others and Hari wrinkled up her nose.

'Great job!' cried Bryony.

'It looks like Piggy!' beamed Will and Emma's face suddenly fell.

'Yes! So cute!' Bryony squeaked. 'And cuddly, and – and – adorable!'

'You're going a bit over the top,' whispered Hari.

'Oh, right.'

They popped back to Seaview to check on the ponies, who were all happily munching hay. Earlier Bryony had helped Abi put out extra hay bales because the grass the ponies usually ate was covered in snow.

When Piggy had *finally* finished his snack he was ready to go back to the farm. Emma said Will could ride him back and she'd hold the lead rein. She'd given her brother an early Christmas present – a nearly-new riding hat as Will had been nagging to learn to ride for ages.

'Have a great ride!' Bryony waved them off. Then she and the others took their ponies in to give them a good brush down. Josh, who'd left his bike against Red's stable wall, went too.

Back in the warm, Bryony dried Red while Josh checked his hay net and water bucket.

'Now let's see those hooves, Red,' Bryony said. Before she'd turned him out she'd given them a good rub with a mixture of Vaseline and cooking oil.

'Great!' said Bryony. After careful inspection it appeared to have worked very well. She only had to pick out a tiny bit of snow, then she brushed Red down until he shone.

'You sleepy?' she asked. He was resting his hind leg, his ears flopped to the side. 'Just one sec while I quickly check your bed.' And she fluffed up Red's straw with a pitchfork.

'There!' said Bryony. 'That'll keep you snug.' And slipping outside, she and Josh left him to rest.

The yard was busy with ponies coming and going. Lessons would continue until Christmas Eve, though the normal happy chatter was getting more and more excited as talk turned increasingly to Christmas!

Hari, Finn and Alice now appeared. Emma was still up with Piggy.

'Fancy coming with us to the post office?' asked Hari. 'We're off to get sweets, and Alice needs bread for her mum.'

'Sure,' said Bryony, and Josh nodded and went to grab his bike.

'On second thoughts,' he said, 'I might leave it here and walk with you lot.'

It took them ten minutes to walk to town. 'Oh, look!' said Bryony when they reached the main street. It was huddled in a thick white blanket of snow.

'It looks just like a Christmas card!' said Alice.

The cobbled streets, the doorsteps, the shop windows, the rooftops – everything twinkled like magic! The houses reminded Bryony of her gingerbread house, with icicles hanging from the eaves. Except – she was very relieved to see – no Tyrannosaurus rex was wedged in any of *these* chimney pots!

Alice bought her mum's bread and they all got sweets – strawberry bonbons and sherbet lemons as Miss Pigeon informed them she was out of spiced apple and cherry jellies.

'Sold them all yesterday, so there!' she nodded, though her breath, Bryony noticed, still smelled distinctly of spiced apples and cherries!

'Now then,' sniffed Miss Pigeon. 'Off you go! I'm shutting as I needs to be somewhere.' And before Bryony could ask *where* she'd flapped them all out of the shop.

They ate their sweets on the park bench, after they'd scooped off all the snow. Then they had a quick go on the roundabout, twirling – thought Bryony – like Meredith!

When they all felt dizzy (and a little bit sick),

they headed off to Alice's house to deliver her mum's loaf of bread. Alice lived just off the town's main street, near Chestnut Lane Primary, their old school. Their new secondary school, Brook Dale High, was great but Bryony had very happy memories of Chestnut Lane.

On their way there they passed the town square where the Christmas Market would be held later on. Grandpa's pal, Cabbage Patch Charlie, was helping decorate a huge Christmas tree.

'Hello, Charlie!' Bryony waved across.

'Hello, young Bryony!' he called back. 'I hope you've been saving your pennies for later?'

'I have!'

The children veered off up Chestnut Lane. But as they passed the school they heard cross voices from inside ...

'How *very* dare you! I's prettier than you!'

'You is NOT!'

Bryony's detective radar was immediately buzzing. 'Hey, it's the two Miss Ps,' she whispered. 'And it sounds like they're squabbling!'

Hari shrugged. 'So? What's new?'

Miss Pigeon and Miss Parsley had fought since

they were girls, over eighty years ago! They mostly fought over who made the best jam. So what could they be squabbling about in the Christmas holidays – *in the primary school* . . .?

'I think we need to investigate,' said Bryony. And before they could stop her she was at the school door. 'Come on!'

They followed her in and along to the hall then slipped inside behind her.

'Oh!' said Bryony. 'The town play meeting!' She and her friends had forgotten all about it what with everything going on at the stables.

'Looks like Mr Pettifour is giving out the parts,' said Finn.

Brook Dale High had already done their Christmas play but the *town* play was quite another thing. Anyone could be in it, young or old. And although it was fun it brought out the worst in some people . . .

'I will *not*!' yelled Miss Pigeon, stamping her bony foot. 'I will *not* be an Ugly Sister! I ain't ugly, not like *some* I could mention!'

She shot a look at Miss Parsley on stage beside her.

'Don't look at *me*, Eliza Pigeon!' roared Miss Parsley, puffing out her cheeks like a bullfrog. 'Huh! At least *I* has all me own teeth! Why, I'm so pretty, I should be Cinderella. Not one of them . . . grr . . . ugly sisters!'

'I has me own teeth *too*!' shrieked Miss Pigeon. 'And if *anyone* should be Cinderella, it's *me* because of me lovely sweet nature!'

'You what?' boomed Miss Parsley.

'I'M KIND!' snapped Miss Pigeon. 'Now kindly shut up! You is making me . . . *less* kind!'

'Silly old goat!' Miss Parsley puffed. '*I'm* the kindest!'

Bryony and the others tiptoed to some chairs and sat themselves down in the back row.

'So, clearly the play's *Cinderella*,' grinned Josh, and Bryony nodded.

Up on stage with the two Miss Ps was Jeremy Pettifour, Chestnut Lane's headteacher. Mr Pettifour was always in charge of the play as he thought himself a bit of an actor. Today he was wearing a black velvet suit, flowery shirt and bright blue beret. He also had a clapperboard, a deckchair with his name on, and a clipboard decorated with tinsel.

Mr Pettifour, Bryony now deduced, must have just given the two Miss Ps the role of Ugly Sisters. She couldn't imagine why he would have put them together when everyone knew the feisty old ladies were always much better kept apart.

'Ladies, ladies!' Mr Pettifour twinkled, flicking back his long floppy fringe. 'Now I'm *sure* we can come to some arrangement. In fact ... oh, yes! I have a *marvellous* idea. Come, come!'

He swept them off the stage to be calmed (by someone else), then gazed down at his tinselly clipboard. 'Now let me see ...'

As he stood there deep in thought, Emma and Will tiptoed in and sat down with Bryony and the others.

'Oh, you remembered, Em!' Bryony whispered.

'Yes!' Emma nodded. 'Have I missed much?'

Bryony glanced across at the two Miss Ps, now 'coming to some arrangement' by the climbing frame. Miss Pigeon was waving her bony fist at the poor teacher trying to calm her down, and Miss Parsley was puffing with a face like thunder.

'Nah, you haven't missed much at all, Em,' grinned Bryony. 'It's all *peace and goodwill* here!'

'Ahem!' clucked Mr Pettifour, flicking back his fringe. 'I shall now give out the remaining parts – and no interruptions, if you please.'

Bryony and the others weren't expecting big parts so there'd be no complaints from them.

A few weeks ago, when they'd signed up for the play, they'd only ticked the 'Extras' box as they'd so many other commitments at the stables. Since Extras weren't needed at all the rehearsals, they'd decided as a group that this would be the best option.

Mr Pettifour began with Cinderella. 'And this,' he announced, 'shall be ... *Alice.*'

'But—' piped up Alice.

'No interruptions, remember – if you please!'

Alice looked at her friends in disbelief. 'But I'm meant to be an Extra,' she whispered.

'Don't worry,' whispered Bryony. 'I'll help with Princess P and you'll be great.'

Mr Pettifour continued, now rattling through the parts and hardly stopping to draw breath for fear of further interruptions. Jed Jenkins got Prince Charming (*if* he promised to behave), Martha Lightfoot got Fairy Godmother, Tabby's mum (the very pushy Belinda-Jayne Tibberthwaite-Browne) got the role of Wicked Stepmother.

'*Probably*,' whispered Hari, 'because Georgina Brook's not here!'

Then Bryony and the others got 'Ball Crowd', which Bryony was really pleased with.

'Yes!' she nodded. 'I'll definitely take that.' Ball Crowd meant fun, few rehearsals and – fingers crossed – a fairly decent gown. Plus, there was scope for her to 'make it her own' in the dance scenes.

She was also relieved that she didn't get 'Pumpkin', so she wouldn't be big, round and orange. Will got that and he was over the moon, so it had all worked out very well.

Now that the parts had all been given out, the first rehearsal could start. Miss Pigeon and Miss Parsley were welcomed back on stage, and Bryony was dismayed to see they'd actually stopped glowering. *Then* she found out why . . .

'Ladies!' Mr Pettifour said to them. 'Thank you for your . . . "enthusiasm".'

'Just spit it out!' Miss Pigeon snapped.

'Yes, right.'

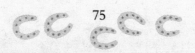

Mr Pettifour flicked back his fringe again and turned to the rest of the cast.

'A small *announcement*,' he twinkled, 'if I may be so bold. We have renamed the role of ...' he lowered his voice, '... the *Ugly* Sisters. They shall henceforth be known as: the *Quite Beautiful* Sisters!'

'No! No! VERY Beautiful!' Miss Pigeon corrected him, and Miss Parsley gave a grunt.

'Too right!'

Mr Pettifour nodded. 'Err – yes, o-of course! And we also need a pony to pull Cinderella's carriage.'

'Tiberius!' boomed Belinda-Jayne Tibberthwaite-Browne, turning a deep shade of magenta. 'Why, Tabby's pony is made for the part! He's smart, and strong, and—'

Mr Pettifour snapped his clapperboard. 'Cut!' he said in a tinkly voice. 'The pony to pull the carriage – I've *decided* – shall be Piggy. It really *must* be Piggy and I shall hear no more of it, as Piggy's the right size for the stage.'

'That's brill, Em!' beamed Bryony, genuinely pleased for her, but Emma had gone ghostly-white. 'He'll be fine,' Bryony nodded.

'*Will he?*' gasped Emma.

'Sure!'

'A-and the final part,' Mr Pettifour announced, 'is that of Stepmother's Cat. I need a right little grump-bag for this.'

'Blueberry Muffin!' blurted Bryony instinctively. Then she clapped a hand to her mouth. But actually it did make sense. Her cat had been a grump-bag ever since he'd been born, but *finally* he had a chance to shine for it.

'Perfection!' Mr Pettifour said with a flourish.

'Blimey,' muttered Josh, rolling his eyes. 'Looks like Berry's in, Bry.'

'Oh, my goodness!' gasped Bryony, glowing with pride. 'He won't let you down, Mr Pettifour!'

Chapter 6

While Mum did the bannister decorations at the Manor that afternoon, Bryony and Josh got to spend some time with Grandpa. They caught the one o'clock bus to Nettleton and on the trip Bryony told him all about the play meeting they'd just come from.

'It was great!' she said. 'After everyone had stopped arguing.'

Grandpa chuckled. 'I see! Did you get a part, Josh?'

'Ball Crowd,' replied Josh, looking up from his comic.

'Me too!' beamed Bryony. 'And, you'll never guess what – Blueberry's Stepmother's Cat! He's got to be grumpy so he doesn't even need any practice!'

Grandpa nodded.

'And *Piggy* is the pony,' Bryony went on, 'who will pull Cinderella's carriage. Mr Pettifour needs to find a good carriage though first, but—'

'Ho-ho!' Grandpa rubbed his hands together. 'I might have just the thing! My friend, Bob, from the Classic Car Club, has got this old motorbike and sidecar. Well, just the sidecar but it could be a real belter with a little bit of TLC. It's a 1915 H-D sidecar rig. Cracking visibility for Cinderella!'

Bryony had a vague idea of what a sidecar rig was as Ebony Swann had travelled in one once. She wasn't convinced it would work though. How would they attach it, for one thing? And Piggy didn't like moving at the best times, let alone pulling a sidecar behind him. But Grandpa looked so excited that she couldn't bear to crush his enthusiasm.

'That sounds, um ... great, Gramps,' Bryony said. 'I'll tell Mr Pettifour – and thanks!'

Around twenty minutes later the bus stopped in Nettleton's high street in front of Clarington's, a large department store.

Nettleton was much bigger than Brook Dale,

79

with numerous cafés and pubs, as well as shops. It even had a sports centre and a cinema with lots of screens.

As Bryony got off the bus, she saw the snow had stopped. The pavements were as snowy as Brook Dale's, but the roads had been gritted the night before so the journey over hadn't been too bad.

Clarington's had a wonderful display in its main window. Little mechanical elves were helping Santa make presents! Each elf was wearing a tiny hat in frosty pastel colours. Mint green, pink, a twinkly ice-blue. And they had cute waistcoats matching the colour of their hats with Christmas decorations on – bells, snowflakes, and best of all, thought Bryony, were the tiny red and white candy canes.

'Oh, wow!' said Bryony. It was all so fun and Christmassy!

'Which café for lunch then?' Grandpa asked.

'One with chips,' replied Josh.

'Right,' said Grandpa. 'The Seahorse it is! Follow me.'

They walked along to a little side street a stone's throw away from the harbour. The pavements were slippery but Bryony soon learned if you stayed in other people's tracks you were fine.

The Seahorse was packed with Christmas shoppers with brightly coloured bags filled with presents. All the tables were taken but then a family left so Grandpa grabbed their table by the window. A few moments later, one of the staff came to clear it. He looked about eighteen and was wearing a Christmas jumper with a great big penguin on the front.

He was also wearing a Santa hat (all the staff were) but his bobble kept slipping down over his face and whopping him on the nose. He didn't seem very happy about this, trudging off with the dirty plates, muttering. And when he came back to take their order, his Santa hat, Bryony noticed, had vanished.

Grandpa ordered scampi and chips all round. 'And see, Josh ...' he said, '... right here on the menu it says we can have "bottomless chips"!'

'What? Chips without *bottoms*?!' Josh said with a snort, and Bryony tutted. When *would* her brother stop sniggering over the word 'bottom'?

'No, it *means*,' said Grandpa, 'if your chips run out, you can have more – free.'

'Chips *run out*?!' Bryony now grinned. 'But surely that's impossible! Everyone knows — that only *runner* beans have legs!'

Everyone was in very good spirits as they tucked into their lunch. The café was decorated with fairy lights and was ever so toasty and snug. And Josh managed three whole portions of chips before finally admitting he was full!

The antique shop they had come to visit was one Grandpa knew very well. It was called 'Thimblefold's Trinkets and Treasures' and was run by a really friendly old man by the name of Samuel Thimblefold. Samuel lived in Brook Dale, in one of the pretty painted fishermen's cottages, just a few doors down from Grandpa's, so Bryony often chatted to him when she was out and about on Red.

She'd also been to his shop a few times before because Grandpa liked antiques. She'd last visited with Grandpa a few weeks ago when he'd spotted a brooch for Mum for Christmas. Samuel, very kindly, had been keeping it aside while Grandpa saved up enough money to buy it. It was a vintage brooch in antique gold with pale-green and turquoise stones. Bryony knew that her mum was going to absolutely love it.

After Grandpa had paid for their lunch, they wrapped up warm before stepping back out into the snowy street. Thimblefold's Trinkets and Treasures was in a narrow lane around the corner.

'Right then,' said Grandpa as they headed off. 'A quick stop-off to buy the brooch then back to the Brook Dale Christmas Market.'

'Oh, yes!' Bryony quickly checked her watch. 'The Market starts at three thirty, doesn't it?'

'Aye,' Grandpa nodded. 'It does.'

'Well, if it's okay with you, Gramps,' Bryony said, 'I'd really like to be there at the start because I've seen what I want to get Mum for Christmas.'

'Not a bracelet from Thimblefold's then?' Grandpa asked. Bryony had told him, after their last visit, that she might get her a silver bracelet she'd seen.

'No, I've changed my mind,' said Bryony. 'I think Mum would love a little moon gazing hare I came across yesterday morning. His name's Hector – or so Meredith said. Her parents made him. They're travellers,' she went on. 'They have this beautiful caravan – a deep reddish-purple with lots of flowers and berries painted on it.'

Grandpa looked thoughtful. 'Hmm, I think I might know it. The mum and dad came before . . . maybe seven or eight years ago, when your Grandma Mathilde was still alive. I bought my Matty a wooden dormouse in a little matchbox from them. Their caravan is pulled by a huge horse, right? And do you still pitch up in the meadow by Bluebell Wood – near the holly?'

'Yes!' replied Bryony nodding back.

'Aye, nice folks,' Grandpa smiled. 'They said they park by the holly as there's an old saying that pitching near holly keeps you safe.'

'Really?' said Bryony. 'I hope that's true. Though most people in Brook Dale are really kind so I'm sure they'll look out for them too.'

'They've got this bear, Gramps too. And he's massive,' Josh chipped in. 'Do you think Mum would buy him for my bedroom?'

'But how would he fit through the door, Josh?!' laughed Bryony.

'Oh, yeah.'

They passed a chocolate shop with chocolate

everything in the window – elves, mice, reindeer and hedgehogs. Josh nipped in and bought a hedgehog for Mum. They put it in a little silver box tied with a snowflake ribbon.

'One present done!' said Josh, heading out. Then he stopped. 'Do you think it's enough though?'

Josh suddenly looked worried. 'The thing is,' he said, 'I thought I had a bit more money saved up. But, well . . . you know.'

'Mum will love it!' smiled Bryony. 'She loves chocolate, and hedgehogs. And hedgehogs have prickles, so that means – more chocolate!'

'Good thinking!' Josh's face brightened at once as he carried on down the street. Grandpa caught Bryony's eye.

'You're a very kind girl,' he whispered.

Next they passed the cheese shop and Grandpa announced that he loved a nice bit of Stilton.

Bryony nodded. *Right!* she thought. That was Grandpa's Christmas present sorted. Later, at the Market, she'd get him a chunk of stinky cheese!

After that came the glove shop. No one was interested in that. Then a shop that sold fizzy bath bombs that looked like cupcakes.

They now turned the corner into Limpet Lane where Samuel had his antique shop. 'Oh!' Bryony stopped. She pointed along the lane.

'What's happening?'

Halfway down, right outside the antique shop, a police car was parked, its bright blue light flashing.

'Do you think something's happened to Mr Thimblefold?!' gasped Bryony.

'Let's go and see!' said Josh.

'No, wait!' Grandpa's voice was unusually firm. 'You two stay here. I'll go.'

Bryony was not one for staying put. But this was different. It felt serious.

The shop was only a few doors down. A couple of shoppers were hovering outside it and Bryony could see that the shop door was closed.

She watched as Grandpa walked towards it, his breath misting the air. He stopped by the door and spoke to the shoppers. One of them shrugged and the other shook her head. They both moved off along the lane, but Grandpa waited.

A few moments later the shop door opened and Bryony saw two policemen walk out. One of them was carrying a large cardboard box.

'What's in the box, Bry?' Josh whispered.

'It looks like lots of silver things,' replied Bryony, edging forward and craning her neck to see. Ebony Swann wouldn't just stay put. She'd be *itching* to have a nose – and so was Bryony!

As well as a very large candelabra, there looked to be several picture frames, a coffee pot, a round tray and a couple of jugs and vases.

'It looks very expensive too,' Bryony said.

One of the policemen opened the car boot and the other placed the box in. Then, as Grandpa stood watching, they got in the car and drove off.

As soon as they'd gone, Grandpa headed into the shop as the policemen had left the door open.

'What do you think's going on?' asked Josh.

'I'm not sure.'

They waited until Grandpa reappeared and beckoned for them to come. As they headed off, it started snowing again. But this time the flakes were big and thick and Bryony found herself shivering.

Pulling her scarf around her, she carried on along the slippery pavement. The sky was suddenly very dark and it looked like a snowstorm might be heading Nettleton's way.

Bryony followed Josh into the shop and closed the door behind them. *Ting ting!* Its little brass bell tinkled and Bryony's thoughts turned again to Mr Thimblefold. *Why* had the policemen taken some of his silver?

'Bryony?' Grandpa called. 'Josh? We're round here.'

'O-okay,' called back Bryony. She looked around but couldn't see through the maze of trinkets and treasures. There were sea trunks and chairs. There were footstools and dressers. There were pictures of sailors, and stern-looking queens, and a tiger in a waistcoat and top hat.

And clocks! There were clocks ticking everywhere! Grandfather clocks, cuckoo clocks and one with a tiny train puffing white smoke – going in and out of a tunnel, round and round.

'A skeleton!' Josh pointed. 'This place is awesome. How come I've never been here before? Bry, I *need* that guy! Forget the bear – Skelly could be my rugby team's mascot!'

The skeleton was sprawled out on a burgundy chaise longue next to a cabinet crammed with jewellery.

'Skelly's looking dead relaxed.' Josh sniggered. 'Get it? *Dead* relaxed. Yeah? As in dead.'

'Josh,' Bryony whispered. 'Stop making jokes. We don't know what's happened to Mr Thimblefold.'

'Oh, yeah,' said Josh. He gave a nod. 'Yeah, sorry.'

In the jewellery cabinet, Bryony glimpsed three tiny picture frames that would be perfect for the Coopers' Friendship Jar. According to the price tag, she could even afford them. But now wasn't the time to think of that, she told herself. 'Come on, Josh.'

They battled on past a tall oak hatstand on which some ancient white nighties (that looked a bit like ghosts) were hanging. Then finally they found Grandpa around a corner in a smaller room – with yet more clocks ticking. There was also an old wooden counter on which stood a shiny black crow. And beside the crow was a large old-fashioned till.

For a moment Bryony watched the crow, unsure if it was real or not. Josh promptly helped her out by prodding it.

'Aw, fake . . .' he groaned, disappointed.

Bryony's eyes were now drawn behind the till

where Mr Thimblefold was sitting on a stool. He looked very pale and was staring into thin air, while Grandpa patted his arm.

'As if I would,' Mr Thimblefold mumbled, unaware that Bryony and Josh were even there.

'As if I'd deal in stolen goods! You know me, Albie.' He looked up at Grandpa. 'I'd never do that. Never! I didn't even know where the silver came from – and I told them policemen that too.'

'Shh, it's all right, Sam,' Grandpa replied. 'Try not to worry if you can. Everyone knows you're as honest as they come.'

'But they won't think that *now*.' Mr Thimblefold shook his head. 'Not any more.'

Bryony had never seen Mr Thimblefold look so upset. A bumbly old man with a white beard and small round spectacles, he usually had a big smile on his face and reminded Bryony of Santa. He always wore colourful silk bow ties too, and very homely tweed waistcoats. And his shoes were so shiny you could almost see your face in them!

But Bryony now saw his 'bow tie of the day' – a bright green one with Christmas puddings on – was lying, undone, beside the crow. And the usual twinkle in his eyes, and cheery smile, had disappeared.

Grandpa looked over to Bryony and Josh. 'Do you think you could go out the back,' he said, 'and make some strong sweet tea for Mr Thimblefold? He's just had a shock and I think it might help.'

'And the door!' gasped Mr Thimblefold, looking over with a quiver. 'Could one of you please go and lock it for me, a–and turn the sign to *Closed*?'

'No, Sam,' said Grandpa softly. 'There's no need for that.'

'But there is.' Mr Thimblefold's voice was a whisper. 'I can't possibly stay open after this.'

His eyes looked very watery behind his spectacles now, and his voice was very thin and wobbly.

'I'll turn the sign and you make the tea, Josh,' said Bryony.

With a nod, Josh continued on down a small dark corridor, and Bryony retraced her steps back through the colourful Aladdin's cave to the door.

When she got there, however, its brass bell was already tinkling. In a flurry of snowflakes, a lady and a small boy hurried in.

The lady's coat was white with snow and her

little boy had the hood of his duffle coat up, his dark green trousers tucked into blue wellies with trains on.

'I'm sorry!' said Bryony quickly. 'But Mr Thimblefold, um – he's not feeling well so he's closing early.'

'Oh dear,' replied the lady. 'I hope he's better soon. How grim getting ill in Christmas week.'

Her little boy had gone over to watch the train clock.

'We can't stay, George,' the lady called to him. She turned to Bryony. 'It's his birthday,' she said, 'on the 28th of December.'

'Oh, wow!' replied Bryony. 'Not long to go then.'

'I know,' the lady nodded. 'He'll be five. That's why I've come today.'

She lowered her voice. 'I'd hoped to get him that train clock. The one he's watching now. George is mad on trains, you see. So I thought I might buy it, then come back to collect it when I'm on my own. You have to be prepared when Christmas and birthdays come at once, otherwise you get in a dreadful muddle, you see.'

'Oh, yes!' said Bryony. Although her birthday didn't clash with any other special event, her mum always got in a bit of a flap, what with her and Josh being twins and Mum having to buy for both of them at the same time. Bryony felt terrible that George's mum couldn't sort his birthday present now. And she could see how train-mad little George was, she herself being just as mad on ponies. But clearly something serious had just happened to make Mr Thimblefold so upset. She didn't feel she could bother him about the clock now. Especially as he'd just asked for the shop to be closed.

George's mum went over and retrieved him. Then they made their way back to the door. As they did Bryony wondered if *she* could sell the clock and arrange for it to be collected. Then she could give Mr Thimblefold the lady's money later on.

'Just a sec!' said Bryony. George's mum stopped and George skipped off to the skeleton. 'I'll see if the clock has a price,' Bryony whispered.

Hurrying over, she checked all round it, even the little train chuffing in and out of the tunnel. But sadly there was no price anywhere.

She returned to George's mum and shook her head.

'Thanks so much for looking though,' the lady replied. 'Do you think the shop will open again over the holidays – any day before the 28th?'

'Um …' Bryony had no idea. 'Fingers crossed,' she said.

George's mum nodded, herded him up yet again and guided him out of the door.

'Bye then,' said Bryony, and they waved from the pavement.

'Let's choo-choo home, Mummy!' giggled George. 'Just like that clock!' And together they shuffled off down the snowy street, hissing.

Bryony sighed as she locked the door and turned the sign around. She couldn't bear to see Mr T so upset, or for George to miss out on his train clock. Last week she had no mysteries to solve but, like buses, they seemed to come in pairs. First Georgina Brook's argument with Amber, and now whatever had happened here. But *this* mystery seemed so serious, and sad, it easily trumped Georgina's. Bryony felt desperate to help sort things out but she didn't have any facts yet.

Turning, she hurried to the back room again where Josh was handing Mr Thimblefold his tea.

'Ah, thank you, Joshua,' Mr Thimblefold said.

'No worries,' replied Josh. 'And, um – here. I found a little chocolate hedgehog in my pocket just now. It might make you feel a bit better.'

Carefully he put it down on the counter, and Bryony glimpsed the snowflake ribbon from the chocolate shop trailing from his trouser pocket.

'Oh, that's so kind of you,' Mr Thimblefold said as Josh went to stand beside Bryony.

'Mum would be proud of you,' Bryony whispered.

'He just ... well, looks like he needs it.' Josh shrugged.

'Now, about that silver, Sam,' Grandpa said. 'Tell me *exactly* what happened ...'

Chapter 7

Bryony perched on a nearby chair to listen to Mr Thimblefold's story, while Josh knelt down on an old Persian rug on the floor.

'Well,' said Mr Thimblefold, from his stool behind the counter, Grandpa still at his side.

'It was like I just told those two police officers – I've no idea where the silver came from. It just, well . . . appeared late yesterday afternoon.'

'Um, when you say *appeared*,' Grandpa said, 'someone must have brought it surely?'

'But that's the baffling thing,' Mr Thimblefold replied. 'You're right! Someone *must* have brought it. But I didn't actually *see* them come or go.'

Mr Thimblefold took a sip of tea which steamed

up his little round spectacles. He wiped them with a small red polka-dot hanky poking out of his top waistcoat pocket. Replacing the hanky, he stroked his long white beard thoughtfully.

'So, Sam,' said Grandpa, 'are you saying that whoever brought the silver just left it here and went? I mean, surely they'd want *paying* for it, wouldn't they?'

'I definitely would,' piped up Josh.

Mr Thimblefold nodded. 'Yes, me too. And so has everyone else in the past. Folk come with their treasures for me to buy – and, if those treasures are legitimate, I pay them. Then I clean, or restore, the things I've bought, and finally pop them in the shop to sell.'

'What does legitimate mean?' asked Josh.

'Not fake,' replied Bryony. She'd once seen an Ebony Swann mystery where someone had robbed a bank vault and replaced the gold bars with fake ones made of metal and sprayed gold.

'Exactly so!' Mr Thimblefold nodded. 'Things that are not imitation. I also check – before I buy – that what I'm offered isn't *stolen property*. The police send out lists of stolen items, you see.' He patted a black folder on the counter. 'And I always keep it up-to-date and check it first.'

Bryony nodded. It all sounded clear and logical – apart from the 'appearance' of the box of silver. This didn't make sense and was niggling away in her mind.

'So, Mr Thimblefold,' said Bryony gently, 'if you don't mind me asking, how did you not see the person who left the silver? Did you leave the shop at any point, and leave someone else in charge?'

'Oh, no.' Mr Thimblefold shook his head. 'No, no, I was here all the time. But like I told the police, who asked the same question, it all happened very quickly at the very end of the day. Oh dear, I'm not explaining this at all well!'

'It's okay,' said Bryony kindly. 'Just take your time.'

With a nod, Mr Thimblefold took another sip of tea, then quietly cleared his throat.

'So here I was, at this very counter,' he said, 'yesterday afternoon, a few seconds after five – I know this as my many clocks had only just stopped chiming. I was sitting counting my takings for the day when *ting ting!* went my little brass doorbell. Clearly I can't see the front door from round here, so I finished totting up my money, which only took a few moments, and then I got up to tootle off to see my customer.'

He picked up the little chocolate hedgehog, then put it down again.

'So what happened next?' Grandpa asked.

'Well, I'd barely taken three steps,' said Mr Thimblefold, 'when *ting ting!* the doorbell went again. *Hmm, either my customer has gone*, I thought, *or now I have two!* So I wove my way round the chairs and trunks, then battled past the hatstand nighties. But when I emerged in the front room, I saw that there was no one there. Through the window the lane looked rather busy – people bustling by under the street lamp – but inside my little shop was as quiet as the grave.'

Bryony shot Josh a look before he said anything about skeletons. But Josh looked concerned for Mr Thimblefold.

'So you went into the front room,' Grandpa repeated, 'there was nobody there, and . . .?'

'And then I saw it!' Mr Thimblefold cried. 'The

box of expensive silver bits and bobs perched on the sofa next to Barry.'

'Barry?' gasped Bryony. 'You said no one was there?'

'No one *was*,' said Mr Thimblefold.

'Then who's Barry?'

'Ooo! Is he the skeleton?' Josh blurted out, and Mr Thimblefold nodded ...

'Barry-the-Bones.'

'So he's a *witness*!' cried Josh, completely carried away. 'Like – Barry saw the whole thing!'

Bryony caught her brother's eye. 'He's dead,' she mouthed.

'Oh, yeah.'

Mr Thimblefold looked as flummoxed as Bryony felt. Why would anyone leave a big box of silver without waiting to be paid for it?

'So my plan,' said Mr Thimblefold, 'was to wait and see if whoever left the silver yesterday afternoon came back for it today. If they didn't come by closing time, I was going to call the police. But then – lo and behold – the police appeared! They said they were checking all the antique shops round about, searching for the box of silver. Its owner must have reported it stolen last night, I expect.'

Mr Thimblefold finished his tea and looked up at Grandpa.

'So you see, Albie, I had nothing to do with it.'

'I believe you!' Grandpa nodded. 'And I bet the police did too.'

'Yes, I think they did,' Mr Thimblefold replied. 'I mean, they've known me for years. But they said I should have called to inform them that it had been left here right away.'

'So, did the police say to close your shop too?' asked Bryony.

Mr Thimblefold shook his head.

'Why not keep it open then?' Grandpa asked.

'Oh, Albie, the whole thing was such a terrible shock!' Mr Thimblefold now got to his feet. 'And people talk ... oh, yes, they talk. Until the police find out who stole the silver and dumped it in my shop, my customers will never believe that I had nothing to do with it.'

Bryony was convinced that Mr Thimblefold was wrong. His customers would be loyal to him. They liked him very much!

But he looked so sad and worried as he gathered up his bow tie that Bryony knew when to say no more.

Mr Thimblefold put on his coat and hat. Then he stepped across to a set of drawers, opened one and took out a small box. It was beautifully wrapped in gold paper with a shiny pale green ribbon.

'I matched the ribbon to the gems in the brooch,' said Mr Thimblefold. 'It's for your Elizabeth.'

'Oh, Albie!' said Grandpa. 'Thank you so much.' Grandpa put his hand in his pocket to get out the money for Mum's lovely brooch but Mr Thimblefold raised a hand.

'No,' he said quietly. 'This is on me.'

'Sam! I couldn't possibly,' Grandpa began.

'Yes ... *please*,' said Mr Thimblefold and Bryony felt her eyes well up. 'You've all been so kind to me today, I will pay for it myself – and I won't hear any more on the subject!'

Mr Thimblefold took out his old brown leather wallet. Counting out the exact money for the brooch, he opened the till and put it in.

'Thank you, Mr Thimblefold,' Bryony said. 'My mum's going to love it so much.'

'Come back on the bus with us?' said Josh.

'*Only*,' said Mr Thimblefold, 'if you have this back.' And he held out the little chocolate hedgehog.

'Give it to someone for Christmas,' he said with a wink.

They made their way to the door very quietly. As Mr Thimblefold stopped to turn off a few lamps, Bryony took Grandpa aside.

'Gramps, I hope you don't mind me asking,' she said, 'but do you think I could quickly buy those?' She pointed to the three tiny picture frames she'd seen for the Coopers earlier.

'You certainly can.' Mr Thimblefold had returned. His voice was quiet but he didn't look offended that Bryony had asked at such a delicate time.

'Oh, thank you!' said Bryony. And although he was reluctant to take her pocket money, it was Bryony's turn now to insist that he did.

They walked back through town, along the snowy streets filled with happy, busy shoppers. The bus was crowded. Mr Thimblefold sat beside Grandpa, and Bryony and Josh sat behind them. Mr Thimblefold seemed quiet and on edge.

Halfway through the journey, 'Folk are *looking* at me, Albie,' Bryony heard him whisper.

'They're not, Sam,' Grandpa quickly whispered back.

'They'll never come to my shop again.'

'They will. Chin up. You did nothing wrong.'

Bryony decided to forget the 'Georgina Brook Mystery'. Who *cared* why she was at the stables last night? 'The Mystery of the Silver' was far more important. Mr Thimblefold's happiness depended on it. He was such a lovely old man, and his shop was so interesting. It had been his life for so many years too . . .

'Josh, we *have* to find out who did it,' said Bryony quietly. 'Who stole and dumped that silver.'

'If anyone can find out, it's you, Bry,' whispered Josh.

'No, it's *us*. The Super Six.' Bryony looked determined. 'I want us to do it together.'

Presents were great, and plays were fun. But Christmas was about more than that. It was about friends, and family, and caring.

*

Back in Brook Dale, snow was falling lightly as the bus dropped them off on the seafront as the town's main street was closed off for the Christmas Market.

'See you later, Gramps,' Bryony said.

'Aye, you will,' Grandpa winked. He popped his hand into his coat pocket and pulled out a couple of five pound notes.

'Here,' said Grandpa, holding them out to the twins. 'Some pocket money for the Market.'

'Thanks, Gramps!' said Josh.

'Are you sure?' asked Bryony.

'Certainly!' Grandpa smiled. 'Now, off you go and I'll see you later on.'

Before Grandpa joined them at the Market he was going to walk Mr Thimblefold home and check he settled okay.

'Bye then, Mr Thimblefold,' Bryony said.

'Yeah, and take care,' said Josh.

'Thank you both for everything,' Mr Thimblefold replied. 'Oh, and Joshua, you make an excellent cup of tea.'

'I ... thanks,' said Josh. He shuffled, looking pleased. 'I put in tons of sugar!'

Bryony and Josh crossed the road and headed

up the snowy hill to town. Bryony breathed in the scent of her special blue scarf that was keeping the chill off her neck. It smelled of past winters and big warm hugs from her dad.

But Josh, quite clearly, had smelled something else as they reached the top of the hill.

'*Burgers!*' he cried. 'Bry, quick before they all sell out!'

They quickened their pace. Snow was falling like feathers and the old-fashioned street lamps were glowing. The white crooked shops patterned with black timbers wove their way up into the dark grey sky and overhung the winding cobbled street. Their snow-covered rooftops, earlier iced smooth, were now patterned with trails of tiny bird footprints. Bryony spotted two fat fluffy robins perched on the post office chimney. Town always looked magical, but especially tonight. 'Josh, I really love this place,' she sighed.

The shops were all open and the lights from their windows cast a dreamy golden glow on the snowflakes. Miss Parsley was in the hairdresser's under a very big dryer.

'She must be getting it done for the

Christmas play,' grinned Bryony. 'As she's a *Very Beautiful* Sister!'

'Uh-oh!' Josh sniggered. 'Wait till Miss Pigeon sees that!'

The closer they got to Market Square, the busier it became. The brass band struck up 'Jingle Bells' as people bustled by, laden down with all kinds of gifts.

The 'Wonder Welly Socks' seemed very popular, judging by all the bags. As did the metal bird feeders in the shape of black cats and squirrels. There was also fudge — *so* much fudge — in cellophane bags tied neatly with bright starry ribbons.

Jed Jenkins then came clumping up, looking pleased. '*Yak socks!*' he boasted, waving a hairy pair right in front of Bryony's nose. 'Fit in me wellies for the play, these will!'

'But you're Prince Charming!' gasped Bryony. 'You can't wear wellies to the Ball!'

'Huh!' said Jed with a determined nod. 'Let Pettifour try and *stop* me!'

He clumped off and Bryony looked around.

'Right, I need to find the wood sculptures,' she said.

'Burgers first!' nodded Josh, and he pointed across the street. 'Over there!'

In front of the butcher's, hanging over the pavement was a red and white striped canopy. Under it, Jacob Jenkins the butcher (son of Jasper the farmer, and father of Jed) was barbecuing sausages and burgers on a big steel drum.

'I'll be quick,' said Josh.

'Go on then,' grinned Bryony.

'Thanks!'

Josh wove through the crowds, and when he wasn't looking, Bryony quickly bought his Christmas present. Nearby was the balloon man selling kits to make animals. Josh had seen him at the gymkhana last spring and had seemed really enthusiastic.

She'd only just got back to the spot where Josh had left her when he reappeared with a burger *and* a hot dog.

'You'll be sick,' laughed Bryony, but Josh passed her the hot dog.

'Here,' he said. 'Your favourite, right? And it's not your Christmas present!' he added.

Bryony beamed. 'Oh, thanks Josh!' He'd even got her onions!

'No worries,' said Josh, looking really pleased with himself.

By the time they reached Market Square they felt happy, and very full.

'Wow!' gasped Bryony, looking around. 'Amazing!'

There were stalls all around the square's perimeter. Above it was a building held up by stone pillars and there looked to be stalls up there too.

'It's like Lapland!' gasped Josh. It was different to last year – even better!

The outside stalls were housed in quaint wooden huts that looked like giant gingerbread houses. They were decorated with strings of twinkling fairy lights, and little wooden stars. Some of the huts had silver hearts around their eaves dangling from gingham ribbons, while others had dried oranges and popcorn threaded onto twine.

Each of the huts was selling something different. 'But how to choose!' laughed Bryony. There were stained-glass robins and bright angels that spun. There were furry earmuffs and teddies on sleighs. There were wooden toy soldiers holding small painted drums, and ballerinas on strings that danced! There was fudge, toffee, Turkish delight and little sugar mice – pink and white, and the prettiest primrose yellow!

Then Bryony saw the Christmas tree at the front of the hall, supplied by the local tree-trimmers. A sign below it said:

DONATED BY
'COPSE AND LOGGERS'
AND A VERY
MERRY CHRISTMAS
TO YOU ALL!

The tree was huge, and covered with tinsel and lights and the daintiest glittery baubles. On the top was a star made from amber-coloured glass which shone like pure gold.

'Not bad!' nodded Josh, looking it up and down with a grin.

Just then, the rest of the Super Six appeared.

'Bry, look!' said Emma. 'I've bought Piggy some spray. It's a detangler for *impossible* manes. I need to get him smart enough to pull Cinderella's carriage.'

'Great,' smiled Bryony. 'And I'll help!'

As the friends chatted about what else they'd seen, two ladies in big furry hats passed by, gossiping about Mr Thimblefold. Mr Thimblefold was right – word *did* travel fast, thought Bryony.

She needed to tell the others about the silver. 'Hey, guys,' she said, suddenly serious. 'We've got an important *new* mystery to solve.'

'What?' asked Finn. So Bryony told them all about it.

Everyone looked puzzled. 'Wait,' said Hari. 'Mr Thimblefold didn't *see* who dumped the silver? And they didn't stay to get paid?'

'That's right,' Bryony nodded.

'Highly illogical,' frowned Finn.

'But it's true,' piped up Josh.

Alice sighed. 'Poor Mr Thimblefold!'

'What a shock he must have had when the police arrived,' said Emma.

They agreed to all think about it overnight and pool their thoughts tomorrow. They had their usual Wednesday meeting planned at Lookout

Towers at five but Bryony was certain they'd see each other at Seaview beforehand.

'Right,' she said. 'Christmas shopping time! Anyone know where the woodcarvings are?'

'Down on the Green,' Alice replied.

'Oh, *please* let Mum's little hare still be there,' said Bryony, gazing up at the moon through the snow.

'He will be!' smiled Josh.

But Bryony wasn't so sure. The rest of the day hadn't exactly gone to plan.

'Fingers crossed ...' she said and nodded hopefully.

Chapter 8

Bryony and Josh set off to the Green through all the beautiful stalls. But they hadn't gone far when they came across a hut covered in ivy and winter roses.

'Mum!' cried Bryony. 'Wow, your stall is the best!' Arching right over the little serving hatch was a garland of holly and mistletoe.

'Thanks!' smiled Mum as a customer appeared and bought one of her hand-tied Christmas posies. It had big bold red and purple peonies, white hydrangeas and frosty green eucalyptus leaves.

'I've sold so many of these,' Mum told the twins. 'And my flowerpots with candles are selling like hot cakes!'

At this, the lady who'd just taken her posy snatched up a flowerpot too. 'And this please!' she said. 'Or maybe I'll get *two* ...?'

'We'll leave you to it, Mum!' Bryony smiled, so happy that things were going well. *Lots more pennies for Mum's florist shop fund*, thought Bryony.

She and Josh headed off, but almost immediately a sudden stinky waft stopped them in their tracks.

'Hang on,' said Josh. 'That smells just like my rugby socks!'

Next door but one to Mum's was Hetty Nibblett's 'Cheese and Chutneys' stall, which was attracting people like flies.

'I need to buy Gramps some cheese,' said Bryony, 'before Hetty sells out of stinky Stilton.'

'Judging by the pong,' said Josh, 'I think she's got some left!'

But everyone was clamouring so Bryony wriggled to the front, her pocket money at the ready. She felt quite bad being so pushy. But this, she told herself, was for Grandpa!

'Can I have that, please?' Bryony shouted above the crowd. 'Miss Nibblett! Yoo-hoo! That last wedge of stinky Stilton there! *Miss Nibblett!*'

'Oh!' Hetty Nibblett gave a sudden jump and seemed all of a quiver. Grandpa had a theory that Hetty was a mouse as she was so twitchy and shy. And, of course, she did sell cheese, he'd pointed out. Josh didn't agree. If she *was* a mouse, he'd argued, she would *eat* the cheese, not *sell* it.

'There!' squeaked Hetty, passing the cheese across in a bag and taking Bryony's clutch of coins.

'Whoa!' said Bryony. The smell was strong enough to knock your socks off! Even Josh's old rugby ones. 'Thanks, Miss Nibblett,' she giggled and Hetty nodded back.

Now Bryony herded Josh straight to the Green. They were almost there when Emma caught up with them.

'I might get Dad a wood sculpture too,' she said.

'Good plan!' Bryony smiled. 'Just *not* that moon gazing hare!'

The Coopers' caravan was parked beside the Green, upon which they'd set out their carvings. In the centre of the big round patch of snowy grass stood Blossom, tied to a giant oak tree.

The stall had attracted a large crowd. Bryony wasn't surprised. The Coopers' little wooden animals were gorgeous. She was pleased for the family, but extra-worried now that Hector would already be sold.

'Come on then,' said Josh, 'let's go and see.' But Bryony raised a hand.

'Wait – they're arguing!'

'Who?' asked Josh.

'I dunno,' replied Bryony. 'A customer – at the stall maybe?'

It was so busy over there that they couldn't see who was shouting.

'Hang on!' gasped Emma. '*I* know that voice. It's Mr Brook.'

They quickly edged through the crowd to the front. 'You're right, Em,' said Bryony. And Georgina's dad sounded furious . . .

'It *had* to be you!' Austin Brook yelled. He was glowering at a man who Bryony assumed was Mr Cooper, Meredith's dad.

Bryony had only seen her mum yesterday over at the caravan. But this *had* to be Mr Cooper because Meredith looked very much like him.

'It wasn't me,' the man replied calmly, looking Mr Brook in the eyes. His dark brown curls were

peppered with snowflakes and he wore a long heavy black coat.

'Oh, Kit!' Mrs Cooper called to her husband. 'Tell him about the sticks!'

She sounded so scared as she stood in the snow, her arm around Meredith who looked tearful and quiet. And Morgan was on her other side, looking cross.

A stone's throw away from Mr Brook, Georgina was looking on with her mum. Georgina looked as neat and pretty as ever in a grey fur coat, smart black jeans and a pair of black suede boots. Her outfit, thought Bryony, made her look like a wolf – especially with those icy blue eyes.

Mr Cooper shook the snow from his curls.

'I took nothing from your land,' he said to Mr Brook, 'save the sticks that blew down in the storm on Sunday night.'

'You took my *silver*!' retorted Mr Brook. 'A big boxful from my house. You—'

'Daddy!' called Georgina. 'Just leave it now! You've got your silver back and I want to go home. I'm freezing!'

'We're not going anywhere,' Mr Brook replied,

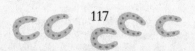

117

'until *he* admits that yesterday afternoon he stole our family silver to sell it to that . . . Thimblefold!'

Bryony gasped. She couldn't believe her ears! So the silver left in Mr Thimblefold's shop *belonged to Mr Brook*!

Even so, thought Bryony, composing herself – he couldn't just go blaming people like this without a single shred of proof! Ebony Swann, she thought, had seen plenty like Mr Brook. Throwing about wild accusations without anything to back them up. It made others miserable. Like Meredith! Only yesterday she'd been so playful and chatty, but now she looked like a frightened little rabbit.

'Mr Brook!' called Bryony, her heart thumping hard. 'You can't accuse people without evidence!'

'Yeah,' nodded Josh.

'It's not how it's done,' said Emma quietly.

Mr Brook glared at Bryony. 'What business is it of yours?' He looked even crosser than before.

'I . . .' Bryony felt the crowd's stare. 'I . . .' But the words weren't coming. Then she thought of her dad. He'd always told her to be brave. Be brave and tell the truth. And the truth was, Mr Brook was being a bully!

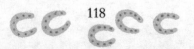

'I think it's everyone's business,' Bryony forced out the words, 'when people are treated unfairly.'

Mr Brook raised his eyebrows. 'Unfairly? Oh, don't you worry, the police will get everything they need.'

He turned to Mr Cooper. 'You haven't heard the last of this!'

Mr Brook marched away in his expensive wellies, his wife and Georgina behind him. Some of the crowd now drifted off too, not buying the wooden sculptures they'd been looking at. But some – Bryony was heartened to see – didn't just take the easy route of blaming strangers and the unfamiliar, and they stayed put . . .

'He's always like that,' said a man to Mr Cooper.

'Take no notice,' called a lady with a pug.

'I think,' said Martha Lightfoot, 'we should focus on these carvings. And *I'm* going to buy this little fox cub.'

'Hear hear!' cried Saul Salmon, the fishmonger. 'And earlier,' he said to Bryony, 'I bought that huge brown bear down at Bluebell Wood.'

'You did?' gasped Bryony.

'Aye,' Saul beamed back. 'Mr Cooper said he's not

quite finished yet, but he'll be ready by Christmas Eve. What a lovely surprise he'll be for me wife. She *did* ask for perfume but ... who doesn't love a bear? I'll need tons of wrapping paper though!'

As he left, Bryony noticed Meredith across the grass. She still looked really sad and was chewing the cuff of her fleece.

'Won't be a sec,' Bryony said to the others. 'I just want to check that Meredith's okay and see if I can still pop round later.'

But it looked like the Coopers were heading off. Mrs Cooper was now walking the children to the caravan while Mr Cooper scooped up the few sculptures not yet sold.

Bryony saw no sign of the moon gazing hare.

'Oh,' she sighed. Well, that was that. Hector had gone to live with another family, even though it had felt like Mum getting him was meant to be ...

As Mr Cooper swiftly hitched Blossom to the caravan, it looked like he wanted to be left alone. The family were now inside, and moments later they were heading off down the road.

As Bryony watched the tracks they left in the snow, Grandpa suddenly appeared.

'I just saw Mr Pettifour,' he smiled, 'and he'd love the sidecar for Cinderella, so I'm going to ring Bob and ask later!'

'Thanks, Gramps,' said Bryony.

'You okay?' Grandpa asked.

'Um, yes!' replied Bryony instinctively.

She glanced at Josh and Emma.

'Well … not really,' Bryony sighed. She just couldn't forget the way that Mr Brook had spoken to Mr Cooper. In front of all these people too. How humiliating it must have been for the whole family!

Plus, they'd never believe a word she said again. After telling them only yesterday how welcoming Brook Dale was, *this* happens!

Bryony only hoped they'd realise Mr Brook didn't speak for the whole town. But no *way* would the Coopers stay for Christmas now. She'd never be the friend Meredith longed for.

'Walk with me,' said Grandpa, taking Bryony's hand. 'And tell me what's made you so sad.'

*

As the Market ended and Mum packed up, Bryony also told her about the scene on the Green.

121

'And I was meant to go and see Meredith now, but I don't know if they'll want me, after that.'

'But you did nothing wrong, love,' Mum answered softly.

'Except tell them that Brook Dale was wonderful,' Bryony groaned.

Mum stopped and hugged Bryony as snowflakes fell around them. The moon was big and bright.

'It *is* wonderful here,' said Mum. 'And they won't blame *you* that Mr Brook lost his temper.'

'But he accused them of stealing his silver,' said Bryony. 'And implied that Mr Thimblefold was up for buying it too – which wasn't true!'

She shook her head.

'Listen,' said Mum, 'Gramps is with Josh, so how about I drive you round to the Coopers'? I'm sure they'll still want to see you. While you're there I could do a few deliveries and collect you afterwards?'

Bryony thought about it. Josh and Grandpa had seen to Red, so she could go right now. Meredith might be expecting her too. And surely she needed to go more than *ever* after what had just happened . . .

'Okay,' Bryony nodded. 'Thanks, Mum. I will go.'

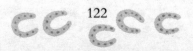

'Come on, then,' said Mum, 'let's get the car. It's starting to get a bit icy.'

Mum was right. As they headed to Bluebell Wood, the roads definitely did feel more slippery, but thankfully they were still okay to drive on.

Mum stopped the car on the lane near the caravan. She told Bryony she'd wait while Bryony checked if the Coopers wanted a visitor.

'Okay,' Bryony nodded. She got out of the car and her feet disappeared into thick snow which went right up to her ankles. Shivering, she headed across the meadow to the caravan, past Blossom tied up under the shelter of the fir trees and draped in a huge warm blanket.

The caravan steps were also covered in snow. She walked up them, her footsteps silent as the moon shone down, and a trickle of wood smoke curled up from the little pipe chimney.

Taking a deep breath, Bryony knocked on the door, her warm breath frosting the air. She waited, and a moment later Mrs Cooper peeped out.

'Oh, Bryony, you came,' she said, looking surprised.

123

'Um, yes,' replied Bryony. 'I'm so sorry about earlier at the Market.'

Mrs Cooper looked very pale in the moonlight, her eyes the most beautiful hazel.

'Would you rather I went?' Bryony asked.

'No.' Mrs Cooper shook her head. 'It wasn't your fault. These things, well ... sometimes happen. And Meredith so hoped you'd come.'

Mrs Cooper now pointed across the little meadow over to the car on the lane.

'Your parents?' she asked.

'Just Mum,' said Bryony quickly. 'She said she'd call back for me after some errands if it's okay with you?'

Mrs Cooper nodded. 'Oh, yes, that'll be fine.'

Bryony turned and waved Mum off, then hurried in through the caravan door.

'It's so cosy!' she cried.

'Hooray!' squealed Meredith, running over and giving Bryony a huge hug. The little girl then seemed very keen to show Bryony around.

On one side was a stove with a crackling fire. And just opposite were some beautifully painted cabinets. Along the back of the van, running underneath the window, was a bed on which Mr Cooper sat, sipping what smelled to Bryony like chicken soup. Beside him, Morgan knelt quietly drawing. A large book was open on the rug. Bryony guessed this was Meredith's favourite 'Alice' story.

'Will you read to me?' asked Meredith.

'I'd love to!' Bryony smiled back. She was so relieved they seemed okay with her coming, and that Meredith looked much more like her bubbly little self than earlier. She was wearing fleecy pyjama leggings and several bright warm tops, the outermost being pink and very fluffy. On her feet were knitted rabbit slippers with cute white pompom tails on the back. And her whirl of dark brown hair was in a long plait ready for bed.

They settled down on the rug and Bryony started to read. As she did, Meredith snuggled up to her, quietly sucking her thumb. Not a single fidget or interruption. She clearly adored stories. Then Morgan appeared too and turned the pages at just the right moment!

When Bryony had finished a whole chapter, Mrs Cooper gave them milk she'd warmed on the stove and buns that tasted of cinnamon. They were delicious! And it was all so cosy and calm.

But then, as they ate, Bryony was sad to hear that the Coopers were thinking of moving on. She wasn't surprised. Who could blame them after earlier? But she wished there'd been time to make *more* happy memories, like this one, before they went.

'Because you'll mostly think badly of the place now,' said Bryony. 'And some people – most people – are kind.'

But even as she said these words, Bryony realised she was asking them to do it again: to *believe* what she was saying.

'Ah, Bryony,' said Mr Cooper. 'We know *you're* kind.'

'Otherwise our Meredith,' Mrs Cooper added, 'wouldn't have chosen you as a friend. You must be a good egg if she likes you!'

'An egg?' snorted Meredith, suddenly getting the giggles. 'Bryony's not an egg!'

'She's a *nag*!' teased Morgan, swiping Bryony's bun.

'Hey! Give that back!' laughed Bryony. Even Morgan was clearly warming to her now.

But despite her smiles, Bryony was sad they

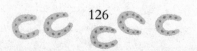

126

wouldn't be around for much longer. She longed to show Meredith the stables and let the twins have a go on Red. The whole family could have come to Plum Cottage for Christmas cake. And maybe told Mum how to make their dreamy buns, if it wasn't an old secret recipe.

As they finished their milk they talked mostly about Bryony, thanks to Meredith's never-ending questions! How she'd felt when she'd first come to Brook Dale. About her mum, her brother, and how much she missed her dad. Even now.

They also talked about Red. How brilliant he was, and how he'd helped Bryony feel part of the place. But how she'd had to give it *time* before things had started to feel better.

The crackle of the stove, the softly falling snow, the silvery moon at the window... For now that was all that mattered. How kind, thought Bryony, of the Coopers to welcome her into their home. And how ashamed she felt that Brook Dale, quite honestly, *hadn't* been so welcoming back.

Heading home in the car, Bryony was thinking hard. This mystery was getting out of hand. Now the Coopers, as well as Mr Thimblefold, had to

Chapter 9

'Can *I* go?' nagged Bryony as she, Mum and Josh were sitting having breakfast next morning. She had tossed and turned all night long thinking about the Coopers and Mr Thimblefold.

'Hmmm,' said Mum. She took a sip of coffee and looked back at Bryony suspiciously. 'I wouldn't have thought you'd have *wanted* to see the Brooks. Not after the Market,' she said. 'If I didn't know you better, I'd think you were up to something!'

'I . . .' Bryony stopped. 'Okay, to be honest, I just want a *tiny* look around the Manor.'

'*Bryony*,' Mum sighed.

'No, listen!' said Bryony. 'About that silver,

well – Brook Dale Manor is the scene of the crime so it's important I have a snoop round.'

'Yeah!' Josh nodded, taking his fourth slice of toast. 'That's what detectives do, Mum.'

Mum put down her coffee cup, folded her newspaper and looked back up at the twins.

'For *one*, Josh,' she said, 'Bryony is not a detective – although I'll grant you she's very inquisitive.'

'In— what?' said Josh.

'Inquisitive!' beamed Bryony. 'Nosy, annoying – all qualities great detectives need. I might actually be a detective one day, I think. Or an *actress*-detective like Ebony Swann. Hey, I think I've just found my dream job!'

Mum grinned. 'But seriously, Bryony,' she said. 'You remember what happened the last time you went creeping around the Manor?'

'Georgina locked you up in the attic!' snorted Josh.

'Yeah. But I wasn't scared,' said Bryony. 'And I'm pretty sure if I go today I won't be locked in *any* of their rooms – so Mum, please?'

'Hey, Mum,' said Josh, annoyingly changing the

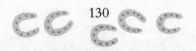

subject. 'Why has Miss Pigeon sent *tons* of toilet paper? Is she trying to tell us something?'

Every Tuesday Miss P sent groceries to Plum Cottage, whether they needed them or not. Sometimes these groceries were nice, normal things. Bread, milk, cheese, maybe fruit – and in nice, normal quantities too. And this usually meant that these were just simple 'groceries'.

Other times, though, she sent 'grocery clues' as to what she'd 'seen in their future'. It was common knowledge that Miss Pigeon thought herself to be a fortune-teller.

Their Tuesday delivery had arrived last night – late because of the Market. And Miss Pigeon had sent *only* toilet paper. Rolls and rolls of it! It was currently on the dresser, piled high. This *had* to be Miss Pigeon giving them a weird clue about something she'd foreseen in their future.

'Okay, so what's she predicting?' puzzled Josh. 'A blizzard maybe? And we'll all get snowed in?'

'And how does that relate to loo roll?' asked Bryony.

'Well, it means that we won't run out!' nodded Josh with a snort.

This sounded rather random, but Bryony had far

more pressing puzzles to solve than why loo roll was taking over the cottage!

'So *can* I go to the Manor, Mum?' she asked. 'Please? It's SO important.'

Mum paused to think. Always a good sign. Now Bryony knew she just had to deploy the 'it makes total sense' line ...

'I mean,' said Bryony, 'it makes total sense. *You* need a cheque for all those lovely displays you've just finished for the Brooks. But you're busy. You're stressed. Work is piling up, right? The pub needs more table decorations *today*. Lavender wants a door wreath and Christmas is creeping up. Like, it's only *three days away* – and—'

'All right, all right! You can go!' puffed Mum.

'Thanks, Mum!' beamed Bryony, gulping down her apple juice and quickly gathering her riding things.

'I'll take Red!' said Bryony. 'He needs a trot out so he'll get exercise and I'll—'

'... get the cheque and *not* snoop round,' said Mum.

Bryony blushed. 'You know me. Fancy coming too, Josh?' she asked.

'Sure,' Josh nodded.

'Great!' Bryony smiled.

They put on their warm padded jackets and headed out. 'Brrr!' Bryony shivered. There was snow everywhere. 'But it seems to have stopped,' she said.

'Yep,' Josh nodded, attempting a wheelie on his bike, only to skid and tumble off. 'We've probably got enough snow anyway,' he frowned. 'It's starting to wreck my stunts now!'

When they got to Seaview, the fairy lights were twinkling and Abi had put a Christmas tree up just inside the main gate. It had clear plastic baubles, and in the centre of each was a photo of each pony who lived there.

Bryony beamed. Red was top centre!

'Cor,' grinned Josh. 'It doesn't get any better than that!'

Just then, a small group of nervous-looking beginners came riding out of the main stable block and down the wide gravelled path to the gate.

Abi was with them, riding Jess's Destiny, while the beginners were on calm, gentle Howie, Megs and Stan, who could be relied on to not get skittish in the snow.

'Hey, Abi!' called Bryony. 'I love the Christmas tree! You finally got round to it then?'

'Not me!' replied Abi. 'Santa's elves must have crept in last night!'

Bryony laughed. 'Ah, I see! And did they leave any play balls too? I'm after one for Red for Christmas.'

'Over in the office,' Abi winked. 'Take your pick.'

Abi led the beginner riders out of the gate and Bryony and Josh carried on to Red's stable. They quickly fed him and mucked him out. Then Bryony gave him a swift brush down, keen to get to the Manor as soon as possible.

As Josh wheeled the dirty straw round to the heap, Bryony tacked up Red. As she did, she told him about her trip to the caravan and the news about Piggy pulling Cinderella's carriage in the play.

''Course I would have chosen *you* to do it,' she said, stroking the little star between his eyes. 'But you don't need to be on stage to be *my* star. You'll always be that, you know? Anyway, I'm glad for Piggy – and Em too.'

Red's ears were forward as he listened, whinnying or blowing in all the right places. Bryony was sure he understood everything she said!

'I need to see Mr Thimblefold later,' she told him. 'To check he's okay and see if he'll open his shop, because the longer he leaves it the harder it'll be."

Bryony patted Red's neck and he nuzzled her arm.

'What?' she grinned. 'You're ready for adventures! Let's have a look at you then.'

Bryony stepped back to admire her work.

'Tack on correctly, coat shiny, hooves oiled and mane and tail tangle-free!'

She nodded. 'And that, Red, is just as well. For *you* are at the top of the Seaview Christmas tree – oh, yes!'

As Red whinnied happily, Josh hurried back in.

'Ready to go then, Bry?' he asked. 'I checked round the others but they're all busy so it's just you, me and Red.'

'Yep!' answered Bryony, putting on her hat. 'Let's do this!'

She led Red outside to the mounting block where Arthur Dobbs was sweeping snow off it.

'I thought you were on snow duty yesterday?' grinned Bryony.

'Yeah, I *was*!' moaned Arthur (secretly loving it). 'And they *tried* to say they didn't need me today but I knew they did really. Best sweeper I am by miles, see? So here I am again,' he rolled his eyes. 'Oh, ALERT!'

A *minuscule* fleck of snow had landed on the mounting block. Arthur swooped down his brush and sent the fleck flying.

'Ha!' he nodded, hitching up his long shorts. 'That'll teach it!'

Smiling back, Bryony quickly mounted Red before Arthur 'alerted' again. As she gathered the reins, Josh pushed his bike towards them.

'Um, you'll never ride that in this snow, Josh,' sniffed Arthur.

'Wanna bet?'

Josh wheeled it out behind Red and jumped on in the lane as he wasn't allowed to cycle in the stables.

'It's quite slippery. But nothing that *I* can't handle,' he said.

Bryony nodded. 'Right, let's get to the Manor.' But at this she could feel Red stiffen.

'It's okay!' She quickly reassured him. He was still very twitchy around Georgina. He probably remembered the bad old days when she'd been his owner.

'I'll be with you, don't worry, Red,' Bryony said. 'And Georgina can't be mean to you any more.'

She squeezed Red's sides and trustingly, he began to head off down the lane.

'So Josh, are you okay to mind him,' asked Bryony, 'if I get inside the Manor to snoop around?'

'Yeah,' Josh nodded as he cycled at her side. 'No worries.'

'I hope I *do* get in,' went on Bryony. 'Because *so* many things about this mystery aren't adding up. Take Georgina, for instance. She was acting really odd down at the Green last night. I mean, she effectively told her dad to move on. Like she wanted to stop the argument.'

'So . . .?' replied Josh.

'That's not like her!' said Bryony. 'Since when does Georgina want to *stop* arguments? Something fishy's definitely going on – and I won't rest until I find out what!'

'Okay, okay, Miss Swann!' puffed Josh. 'Blimey.'

137

Bryony quickened Red's pace. The ride would take them ten minutes. The sun was shining now and the roads, although snowy, weren't nearly as bad as they should have been. Farmer Jenkins, thought Bryony, must have been out gritting in the night.

She had never known anyone whose hobby was 'gritting' until she'd met Jasper Jenkins. He'd grit in all weathers (even a heatwave), was rumoured to have breakfast with a goat, and he and his wife knitted strawberries *for fun*.

His grandson, Jed, had inherited Jasper's love of crazy animals. Bryony hoped that in the play, when Jed was Prince Charming, he didn't suddenly whisk his pet goat from the wings to pull Cinderella's carriage instead of Piggy. For one thing Goaty McGoatface was nibbly. And for two – he butted!

The Manor looked breathtaking when they arrived and Bryony couldn't help but admire it. The vast front garden was elegantly draped in snow.

Red trotted in through the main gate and continued up the sweeping driveway. Emma's dad and Will were *still* planting fresh rose bushes. They waved and the twins waved back.

Bryony brought Red to a halt near the smart front door and Josh squeaked to a stop beside them.

'Well done, Red.' Bryony patted him. 'Now, remember what I said, don't be scared.'

He blew softly, his breath misting the air. He seemed to be okay. He was standing nice and steady and felt relaxed.

Bryony dismounted and Josh got off his bike and went across to hold Red for her.

'Be careful in there, Bry,' he said as Bryony headed up the steps. She turned and nodded back.

'I will.'

Bryony stopped at the door and banged the huge brass knocker. If Mr Brook answered she'd never get inside, particularly after the Market. But Bryony was relieved to see Mrs Brook open the door. Arabella Brook was by far the nicest member of the family.

'Oh, Bryony,' said Bella. 'I was expecting your mother. Are you, um ... okay?'

'Yes, thank you,' answered Bryony. 'Err, how are you?'

This did feel weird after last night, but Bella and Bryony had always got on well.

Bella shrugged. 'Well, you know ... it's been

139

a rather tricky few days. But thanks very much for asking.'

She looked really elegant in a dark orange silk dress, and her hair was in its usual glossy side bun.

'So your mother,' continued Bella, 'is . . .'

'. . . busy with more orders,' said Bryony quickly. 'So I came to collect her cheque instead.'

'Oh, yes,' said Bella. 'Of course – I see. Do come in then.'

Bryony stepped into the magnificent hallway where a vast Christmas tree towered to the ceiling and Mum's bannister decoration looked stunning.

Bella went off to get the cheque and while she did Bryony's eyes darted around, not sure what she was actually looking for. Some clues. *Any* clues! But as far as she could see everything was in its place and as it should be.

Bella returned holding the cheque, which she promptly handed to Bryony.

'Thanks,' said Bryony. And with a smile Bella went to open the front door.

Arghhh! thought Bryony. *No! Not yet!*

She hadn't seen a *thing* to help the investigation. She had to *stay*. Get further inside. But how?

Chapter 10

Bryony's eyes were then drawn to a dresser by the stairway filled with a display of expensive plates. Very different, she thought, to the mountains of loo roll stacked up on Plum Cottage's dresser!

'Wait – *loo!*' gasped Bryony. Yes! That was it. Her ticket for staying longer to snoop. Good old Miss Pigeon, thought Bryony. She'd done it again!

'Sorry, dear?' said Mrs Brook, her hand on the doorknob. 'Did you say something just then?'

Bryony took a deep calming breath. She had to play this cool and look normal ...

'Can I please use your toilet?' Bryony asked politely.

'Oh, yes – of course,' Mrs Brook nodded back. 'They're all working again now, thank goodness! I was beginning to worry we'd all be needing chamber pots soon!'

With that Hari's joke flashed into Bryony's mind about Georgina's '*bone china chamber pot*'. She imagined Georgina flinging it to the floor, looking thoroughly disgusted!

'Pfff!' An impish – and most unhelpful – snort came flying from Bryony's nostrils. She could feel another little menace on its way. She *couldn't* get the giggles. Not now!

Screwing up her face, Bryony clenched her fists to force the second snort to stay put!

'Goodness!' gasped Mrs Brook. 'Are you all right, dear?'

'I . . .' squeaked Bryony, very hot and fists still clenched. She must have looked *desperate* for the loo.

She nodded back quickly, holding her breath as the second impish snort was still hovering around her nostril hair.

'Um – this way, dear,' Bella spluttered. 'Quick!'

Bryony was whisked across the hall and down one of the passageways. She passed a door on her left, which she knew to be the library since she'd been to the house before.

The next room along, though, she wasn't familiar with. On her previous visits the door had been shut. Now, though, it was open and she saw it was a study with dark blue walls and a big oak desk. On the desk she momentarily glimpsed a box. This was definitely something worth investigating! It looked roughly the same size as the one she'd seen the police carry out from Mr Thimblefold's shop. The one containing the Brooks' family silver.

'Here we are!' said Bella at the next door along. 'A splendidly working loo! Come and find me when you're done and I'll see you out.'

Bryony nodded. 'Yes. Find you. Thanks! I ... yes.'

A concerned-looking Bella walked off, but as soon as she'd gone Bryony hurried through the study door—

'Bother!'

In her haste, a packet of Polo mints had tumbled from her jacket pocket. It hit the wooden floor and exploded, mints rolling here, there and everywhere.

'Oh, no!' She had no time for this. Dropping

to her knees, Bryony crawled about after them, stuffing them back into her pocket. This sort of rubbish never happened to Ebony Swann!

When every last Polo had been rounded up, she continued across to the desk.

The study was immaculate and Bryony knew she must leave everything *exactly* as she found it. Miss Swann was always careful to leave no clues that she'd been snooping.

Bryony examined the box, but was annoyed to see it was all sealed up with parcel tape. On top was an address and Bryony deduced it was packed up ready to be posted.

She read the address, written in black ink – presumably by the ink pen nearby:

Cuthbert and Fig
Pudding Lane,
LONDON
EC3R 8AB

'Right.' Bryony nodded, thinking hard. It did look exactly like the box the police had taken. So could she assume that the silver was inside?

Ebony Swann said one should never just assume, but gather as much evidence as possible. So Bryony picked up the box to feel its weight.

It was heavy. 'Hmmm, silver is heavy,' she muttered. Especially lots of it . . .

Next she jiggled it but heard no clatter of jugs, bowls and picture frames. But expensive silver objects, she quickly decided, might well be wrapped individually to stop them bashing about on their journey.

She carefully replaced the box, her brain whirring away. Why would Mr Brook post his family silver off when he'd only just got it back? And who were these people he was sending it to? This Cuthbert and Fig in Pudding Lane?

On a corner of the desk was a desk lamp, its light shining down on a notepad. Beside it was a carriage clock and the smart silver ink pen. On the pen's barrel were the initials 'AB', which probably stood for Austin Brook, Georgina's dad.

Bryony's eyes were drawn to the notepad on which Mr Brook had scribbled down a price. Beside this were the letters 'P' and 'R'. And a word written in capital letters: 'LAPADA'.

Just then, the clock on the desk whirred and chimed and Bryony became aware of the time. She needed to go and find Mrs Brook – now.

Bryony crept back out of the study, only to hear voices in the hall. She listened. It was Georgina and her dad. And it sounded like they were heading her way!

Instinctively she dashed into the loo, shut the door and locked it behind her. She'd be crazy to pass up the chance for some serious earwigging!

She waited. She heard their footsteps growing louder. Louder and louder, until they stopped.

'Georgina,' Bryony heard Mr Brook say, 'have you been in my study this morning?'

'No,' replied Georgina.

'So why's there a Polo mint on the floor by the door frame? It isn't mine.'

Bryony wrinkled up her nose, inwardly groaning. How *could* she have missed that sweet? Ebony would *never* have made such a silly mistake!

'That's strange,' said Georgina. 'I don't give Beau Polos. But maybe the staff do when they groom him? Anyway, Daddy, like I was saying, I'm so very sorry for the way I've been behaving. And I'm *totally* going to be nicer in the future.'

Mr Brook grunted.

'I really am!' said Georgina. 'And I now completely understand why you said before I couldn't go skiing. Although they do still have a *few* places left (according to Camilla) if you *did* believe I'm sorry for the tantrums and ... little accident with the roses.'

Huh! thought Bryony. *Little accident?* Every single rose had lost its head!

'No pressure though, Daddy,' continued Georgina in her super-understanding voice. 'Whatever you decide about the ski trip (which *still* has places on) is absolutely fine by me. I mean, I'm sure the school won't think I'm not going because, say ... we couldn't *afford* it. And Camilla is bound to take tons of photos that *her* daddy can show you and Mummy at your next lovely dinner party!'

There was silence. *Checkmate!* Bryony thought. Georgina, very cleverly, had just gone and pressed all of her father's biggest worry-buttons ...

People thinking they couldn't *afford* something.

Others having news at *his* parties.

And Camilla having something that his daughter did not: a fancy holiday – *with photographic evidence*!

Sure enough, a second later . . .

'Um, *well*,' said Mr Brook in a much softer tone. 'Now that I come to think of it, I might have been a tad hasty before – about the ski trip, I mean. If your *friends* are all going . . . and you *are* truly sorry, then I suppose you really should go too. A–and I'm sure Great–aunt Agatha will completely understand when you're not here.'

'Oh, but *no*!' cried Georgina in the tone of *I couldn't possibly*!

'Yes, yes!' insisted Mr Brook. 'I'll phone the school now. Get it paid today. And I'll get you a new phone with a *much* better camera on. Take lots of photos, won't you?'

'Of course!' cried Georgina. 'I totally will! Thank you, Daddy!'

Well that was that, Bryony thought. No clues here. Just Georgina being Georgina and getting everything she wanted.

Bryony waited for them to go. But suddenly – to her horror – the loo doorknob started to turn. Then the whole toilet door started rattling!

'Daddy!' yelled Georgina. 'The silly door! It's jammed!'

'Let me see,' said Mr Brook. 'Step aside.'

Bryony stepped back too as the door rattled even louder. Not only were they going to tear it off its hinges, but then they'd discover *her* inside!

'Oh, no!' she gasped frantically. What to do?

Then suddenly Miss Pigeon's loo roll delivery flashed into her mind yet again.

'Bad tummy!' hissed Bryony under her breath.

Yes! When she was discovered by Georgina and her dad, she'd pretend she'd had a very bad tummy. So bad it had kept her in the loo for *ages*. Mrs Brook would probably even back her up after earlier!

Grabbing the end of the toilet paper, Bryony pulled off a great long ream. Metres and metres of it! But she *had* to. She had to make it look like her tummy had been so bad that she'd used up nearly all of their paper!

'But whoa!' Bryony stopped and her eyes grew wide. She hadn't thought this through. Where was she going to *put* the loo paper now? It was far too much to flush away. 'Uh-oh . . .'

'Wait, Georgie! I'll get a screwdriver,' she heard

Mr Brook say. He really *was* going to take the door off! Bryony had to get out of there – fast!

Panicking, she quickly unzipped her jacket and bunged the mountain of loo roll inside. When she finally managed to prise the zip back up, she looked like a giant Christmas pudding!

She shuffled towards the toilet, leaned over and flushed so the Brooks could hear someone was in there. *Now* she just needed to step out and deploy her best acting skills.

Bryony tried to turn the key in the lock, but it was stiff and refused to move. 'Oh, you are *kidding*!' she groaned at it. 'Why now?'

'Daddy!' she heard Georgina shriek. 'Someone flushed – and then rattled the key!'

Bryony tried the key again, more forcefully, but *still* it would not budge.

'Who's in there?!' shrieked Georgina.

'It's, um . . . me,' gulped Bryony.

'Who's *me*?'

This was not going well. Mr Brook then returned and, seconds later, the lock was in bits and the toilet door finally open.

Mr Brook and Georgina were – for once in

their lives – completely lost for words. They just stood there, mouths gaping, staring at Bryony, who squeezed herself out of the door, red-faced and massive . . .

'Do *not*,' she said, rolling her eyes, 'eat a *single* sprout for Christmas! Last night, sprout pie for supper – *bad move*.'

And turning, she waddled off down the passage as fast as her legs could carry her!

*

When Josh had *quite* finished laughing, they went to see Mr Thimblefold. Bryony was desperate to check on him after yesterday.

It was snowing again, but only very lightly. The fishermen's cottages along by the harbour were looking as pretty as ever. They were all painted different colours and Bryony's favourite often changed. In the olden days, so the rumour went, the colours helped fishermen to find their own cottage when returning home in the dark. Bryony didn't know if this was true. But Mr Thimblefold's was Santa-red so you could certainly pick out that one!

'How kind of you to come,' the old man said,

seeing Bryony on his doorstep. He was still in his dressing gown and slippers, even though it was almost mid-morning. And his long white beard didn't look as neatly combed as usual.

'Are you feeling better?' Bryony asked.

'Oh, yes, much better,' he quickly replied. But Bryony wasn't so sure. *She* often tried to put a brave face on things too.

'Hi!' called Josh, holding Red in the lane.

'Oh, hello, Joshua.' Mr Thimblefold waved back. 'And let me come and see Red.'

He followed Bryony back and patted Red's side.

'Aren't you lovely, eh?' he said, and seemed delighted when Red nuzzled his shoulder.

'He likes you,' said Josh. But despite his smiles, Bryony didn't think that Mr Thimblefold looked himself.

'Mr Thimblefold,' she said, 'I was just wondering, are you opening your shop today? I expect lots of people still want presents.'

She was about to tell him about little George who'd *adore* the train clock for his birthday, but that would be unfair pressure, she decided, and stopped herself.

Mr Thimblefold shook his head. 'I'm a little tired today. And ... it's chilly. I'd best get back inside.'

He turned back towards the house.

'Um!' blurted Bryony, and Mr Thimblefold stopped.

'Yes, my dear?'

Bryony didn't want to push, but the sooner she could help, the sooner things could get back to normal.

'I don't suppose you've remembered anything more, have you? About Monday afternoon?' she asked gently.

Mr Thimblefold shook his head again. 'I just remember the bell tinkling and walking into the front room. The box of silver was there. And through the shop window the street lamp was on, and ...'

He paused for a moment, stroking his beard and thinking very hard.

'... And I saw a few people pass by in the street. A lady in a headband – it was furry, I think. And a man in a beanie hat with ginger hair. Oh! And a big group of *penguins* went waddling by.'

'Penguins?' Josh frowned, and Mr Thimblefold nodded.

'Not real ones,' he added. 'Just children dressed up. Hurrying home after their school play, I'd imagine.'

With a nod he wandered back to his cheery red house and stepped in through the front door. Bryony went to wave but then she paused. 'What's that?'

A low distant rumble, like the sound of angry bees, had suddenly filled the air. Mr Thimblefold had heard it too. So had Red, whose head jerked back so fast he might have bolted had Bryony not been there.

'It's all right, boy,' she said, keeping hold of his reins. 'Nice and steady.'

As Red settled again Bryony looked down the lane. The angry rumble was growing in volume. But then she saw it was just Farmer Jenkins on his tractor, which he stopped outside Grandpa's.

Gritting again, was Bryony's first thought. But hooked to the back of the tractor, Bryony then saw a trailer. And in it was what looked like a giant tin shoebox on wheels!

'Why!' gasped Mr Thimblefold, peering through his small round spectacles. 'If I'm not mistaken that's an old sidecar. A vintage one too, I believe.'

'Morning, Sam!' nodded Farmer Jenkins, jumping down from his tractor.

'Oh, yes! Good morning, Jasper.' Mr Thimblefold waved.

Farmer Jenkins thumped up to Grandpa's door like a big gentle giant, two trails of grit spilling out of his trouser pockets behind him.

Bryony swiftly mounted Red to get a better view. This sidecar, she thought, had to be the one that Grandpa had been on about yesterday. The one he was borrowing off his friend Bob – for *Cinderella*.

Poor Alice! She'd be going to the Ball in a *shoebox*. But it was so kind of Grandpa to ask Bob, and for Bob to lend it to them too.

Maybe Alice would think it 'charming' in a quirky kind of way, Bryony hoped to herself. But actually, how would they attach it to Piggy? He wasn't a motorbike!

Suddenly Grandpa came out. 'How marvellous!' he cried, and Farmer Jenkins nodded back brightly.

'And Sam!' Grandpa called to Mr Thimblefold, seeing him peeping from his doorstep. 'I shall certainly need *your* help with this.'

'How so?' Mr Thimblefold called back.

'Well,' said Grandpa, 'Bob said it needs repairing. And we've hardly got any time. So what with all the stuff you've fixed in your shop, I'll need to pick your brains. Then I've got this good wax when it's back in one piece, to shine it up.'

'Oh,' said Mr Thimblefold, a small twinkle in his eyes. 'Yes. Well, I do like repairing.'

'Of course you do!' Grandpa smiled. 'So how about we start now as you're at home today? Better than doing nothing, eh?'

Mr Thimblefold hesitated. 'I . . . could help,' he said slowly.

'Perfect!' beamed Grandpa. 'Get washed and dressed and come round then!'

Grandpa winked at Bryony who winked back. That was such a kind thing he'd just done! Grandpa could *easily* fix the sidecar himself but knew that, right now, Mr Thimblefold needed something to help him through his sadness.

But Bryony needed to help him too by solving

'The Mystery of the Silver'. Then his wonderful shop could open again and Mr T could wear his jolly bow ties – and sell brooches, and skeletons, and tigers in top hats. And clocks with little trains, just right for birthdays ...

Chapter 11

'Come *on*, Josh!' called Bryony at two minutes to five as they hurried through the Lavender Lighthouse Tearoom to the dark blue door behind the counter. This door was only used by the Super Six as it led the way up to their mystery-solving den in Lookout Towers.

There were lots of stairs to the room at the top, and like everything here, they were circular. Bryony went first and Josh followed behind as the stairs were steep, dark and narrow. As she climbed, Bryony imagined all the boots that must have trodden these stone steps before hers. Old lighthouse keepers! What a thrill they must have felt, climbing up on black stormy nights to the beacon of safety – the dazzling light at the top!

She imagined them peering through windows in the sky as waves hammered the rocks far below. Brave. Selfless. Watching for others, as charcoal-grey clouds snuffed out the moon's silver rays . . .

'Ha! I'm dizzy!' Bryony gasped as she took the final steps at a run. She didn't want to waste a single second. Mr Thimblefold and the Coopers – they all needed her. They might not have boats being buffeted in storms, but still they were sinking in sadness.

'Not so fast!' Josh called from behind, his voice apprehensive. Although he loved the idea of a den in the sky, he was really nervous of heights.

The stairs led to a hatch up into the top room. This was the room where the light had shone when the place had been a working lighthouse. It still had the light and, although now not used, Bryony still found it captivating.

She climbed up through the hatch, followed by Josh. The rest of the Super Six were already there, sitting on cushions and beanbags, chatting.

'Hi!' said Bryony.

'Here, Bry,' called Emma. She'd saved Bryony's

usual cushion beside her, near the circular window. Josh's favourite beanbag was waiting for him too, but further into the room as he preferred to keep his distance from the windows!

Bryony sat down. It was starting to get dark and this made Lookout Towers feel extra snug. Snowflakes were swirling past the windows and Bryony could hear the waves pounding the craggy headland on which the lighthouse stood.

As well as cosy cushions and big squashy beanbags, Lavender had looped bunting around the walls and dotted lanterns about the floor. They were battery ones for safety, but looked just like the real thing.

As Bryony gently broke the news to Alice that she was going to the Ball in a sidecar, the hatch at the top of the stairs opened and Lavender's head appeared.

'Yoo-hoo!' she called, coming up with a tray. She always brought them treats for free.

'Milkshakes!' cried Josh. There were cakes too, and sandwiches.

'Thanks!' came a chorus of voices.

Smiling back, Lavender put down the tray. 'I'll

leave you to it, then,' she said. 'Mystery-solving on an empty stomach never works!'

She left, and everyone grabbed a cake and opened their mystery-solving notebooks.

'Okay, Case 7,' Bryony began. 'The Mystery of the Silver. Has anyone had any more thoughts?'

She waited, pencil poised. But no one said anything.

'Well, earlier,' continued Bryony, determined to crack on with whatever they had, however small, 'I thought Mr Thimblefold had remembered something. But it turned out he hadn't.'

'Nothing?' said Hari.

'Nope,' sighed Josh. He sipped his chocolate milkshake and shook his head. 'The only thing Mr T added is that he saw some random people passing by.'

'When?' asked Alice.

'Monday night,' replied Josh. 'Just after the silver had been dumped.'

Finn nodded. 'Okay, let's go with that for a sec. Like who?'

Josh screwed up his eyes. 'Oh, no! I forgot.'

'A woman in a big furry headband,' said Bryony.

'A man in a beanie hat with ginger hair. Oh – and some penguins,' she added quickly.

'Penguins?' repeated Alice.

'Oh, yeah,' said Josh. 'He said he thought they were kids dressed up. So that's all we have to go on.'

Everyone quickly jotted down these things.

'What about the Manor though, Bry?' asked Alice. 'Get any clues there? What happened?'

'She got locked in the loo, that's what!' snorted Josh and there followed a flurry of muffled sniggers.

'Thanks, Josh,' tutted Bryony. He'd never let her live that down!

'And as a matter of fact I *did* get a clue.'

'Spill the beans, then!' smiled Hari, pencil at the ready.

'I saw a box,' continued Bryony. 'On Mr Brook's desk. I think it had the family silver in it.'

At this the others suddenly looked serious.

'Did you *see* the silver?' Emma asked.

'Not *exactly*,' said Bryony. 'The box was sealed but I'm pretty sure it was inside.'

'Ooo! Well, give us some box facts!' Alice piped up. 'Its size?'

'Big.'

'Its shape?'

'Rectangular.'

'So, *box-shaped*!' nodded Alice, now looking at Bryony as if they'd just made a major discovery.

'Well . . . yeah,' replied Bryony. But she couldn't help but feel they weren't actually getting very far.

But at least, she quickly told herself, everyone was taking it seriously now, all drawing a picture of a box-shaped box in their notebooks.

'And I'm putting a bow on mine,' Alice beamed.

'Irrelevant!' Hari cried.

'Yes, I know,' smiled back Alice. 'But it does look really pretty!'

When everyone had finished (and Alice had coloured hers in), Emma raised a hand.

'Did the box have an address on, Bry?' she asked.

'Yes,' Bryony nodded. 'I memorised it too. It was being sent to some people called Cuthbert and Fig, and they live in a street in London called Pudding Lane.'

Everyone scribbled down the names and address. Though Josh, Bryony saw, was now drawing a massive trifle.

'Are you taking this seriously, Josh?' asked Bryony.

'Sure!' Josh looked a bit crushed.

'But . . . you're drawing a trifle?'

'I know,' nodded Josh. ''Cos trifle's my favourite pudding. It's like . . . code.'

'So anyway,' said Hari. 'Was there anything else on Mr Brook's desk?'

'Yes – a clock,' replied Bryony, 'a desk lamp, a pen – and a notepad with a word on it in capital letters: LAPADA.'

Everyone noted down the word, Bryony carefully spelling it out.

'I wonder what that means?' Emma scratched her head.

'Hmm,' Finn nodded. 'Me too. I once read a book on ciphers and acronyms, and—'

'Whoa!' cried Josh. 'What are *those*?'

'Well, ciphers are codes,' Finn explained.

'Like my trifle?' asked Josh.

'I suppose,' nodded Finn. 'And an acronym,' he went on, 'is a word whose letters stand for something else, each letter being a word of its own.'

'So you think LAPADA stands for something else?' asked Hari.

Finn nodded back. 'It might.'

164

'Oh!' said Josh, and he silently mouthed something, counting on his fingers as he did. 'Like – Lions Always Pounce After Doughnuts ... um ... Actually. Is *that* an acro-thing, Finn?'

'It is.' Finn nodded.

'But maybe,' grinned Hari, 'not *quite* the right one for this case!'

They carried on thinking and trying things out, but nothing sounded right. When their notebooks were half full of crossed-out scribbles, Josh tried a different tack ...

'Or LAPADA might be something to do with LAPLAND!' he said after polishing off the last mince pie.

'But Cuthbert and Fig can't be *elves*!' snorted Alice.

'Oh, guys,' groaned Bryony. This was hard.

She sat for a while thinking and chewing her pencil. Then suddenly she recalled another clue.

'And Mr Brook's notepad had a *price* on it!' she cried. 'Above two *more* letters: P and R.'

'Princess and Red!' Alice blurted without thinking and suddenly everyone (except Bryony) got the giggles.

'Petunias and Roses!' Hari snorted.

'Peter Rabbit!' piped up Josh.

'Possums on Roller-skates!'

'Pimply Radishes!'

'Properly *Ridiculous* ideas!'

'Right!' called Bryony.

'Nah, that's *not* right,' corrected Josh. 'You didn't do a "P" before it, Bry.'

Bryony sighed. 'I mean right, as in – we're done! I hereby call this meeting to a close.'

'Oh, right,' said Josh. 'Um, sorry we messed about.'

And the others all apologised too.

'Nah, it's okay,' Bryony replied as everyone began to pack up. 'You tried. It's hard. I think we need to sleep on it. But you *will* all think about it tonight, yeah?' Everyone agreed that they would.

'Oh, and don't forget Georgina's odd behaviour!' added Bryony. 'The two cases are probably not linked at all, but her argument with Amber at the stables is still bugging me. And since when does Georgina shut down arguments, like she tried to do at the Green?'

Bryony closed her notebook. 'We *have* to solve this case – really fast. The Coopers are thinking of moving on now and I can't bear them to leave so sad. And poor Mr Thimblefold, we have to help him too!'

'You'll work out the case in the end, Bry,' said Emma. 'We'll help too, but everyone knows if anyone can sort it, it's you.' She patted Bryony's arm.

'Thanks,' replied Bryony quietly.

While every started to file down the hatch, Bryony gazed through the window. Her brain was in a whirl just like the tumbling snowflakes.

Who stole the silver from Mr Brook?

Who dumped it in Mr Thimblefold's shop?

Why dump it?

And why *there*?

Bryony didn't know.

But she did know one thing: this case was not going to beat her! Sometimes mysteries were like that, she thought. Like Piggy's mane – they just needed very patient detangling . . .

*

Red was very happy to see Bryony that night and she was so glad to see him too. He was so loving, and such a good listener.

As she brushed him down, Bryony told him

all that was on her mind, and he replied with soft reassuring snorts, his eyes twinkling.

When Red looked immaculate and was nibbling hay, Bryony decided to nip to the office as she still hadn't bought him his Christmas present – the play ball.

The yard was busy with ponies coming back in. As Bryony passed Tiberius's stable, Tabby was picking the snow from his hooves, whilst practising her lines for the play. Her mum had originally been given the part of Wicked Stepmother but had persuaded Mr Pettifour to let Tabby have it instead because he wouldn't use her pony to pull the carriage.

'Cinderella!' Bryony heard Tabby shriek. 'You shall NOT go to that ball. You must stay right here and sweep the heart and kindle instead!'

'Cut!' cried Mrs Tibberthwaite-Browne. 'We've been over this *so* many times, Tabs. Not *heart* and *kindle* – it's sweep the *hearth* and *cinders* – otherwise she'd have been called Kindle-ella!'

Giggling, Bryony carried on to the office, chose Red's ball and left the money for Abi. She was just heading back, when who should she see but Amber Stepney bringing in Dash for the night.

Bryony still didn't know what Georgina had wanted with Amber last Monday night. She didn't know Amber well enough to ask her either.

But with Amber tonight was her younger sister, Jasmine, who sat by Bryony in History. If she chatted to Jasmine about school, thought Bryony, maybe she could somehow get onto the subject of Amber and Georgina . . .

'Hey, Jas!' called Bryony.

'Hi, Bry!' Jasmine waved.

Jasmine left her sister, who carried on with Dash, and walked across to Bryony.

'I don't usually see you here,' Bryony said.

'Nah,' replied Jasmine. 'Ponies are more Amber's thing. But it was either stay home alone or come here.'

Jasmine's hair was bright ginger like her sister's, but she was much smaller than Amber. Bryony chatted to her for a bit about school, but just couldn't get a link to Georgina and the argument the other night.

Getting rather frustrated, Bryony then had an idea.

'Um, Jas,' she said. 'I was just wondering, have you ever been over to Brook Dale Manor, that big posh house with all the land?'

'Yeah, once,' nodded Jasmine. 'To watch Amber in the gymkhana. Why?'

'Err, well . . .' went on Bryony, still thinking on her feet. 'You know how in History we do projects about old stuff? Well, if we ever did one about an old house, we could maybe go to Brook Dale Manor because that's old and it's got tons of history! W-we could even ask Georgina Brook – um, she's the girl who lives there – all about the old place. Do you or your sister know her?' asked Bryony.

'N-no.' Jasmine slowly shook her head. 'I know of her but that's about it.'

'What about Amber, though?' Bryony said quickly. 'Does *she* know Georgina? Oh! Now I come to think of it, I'm sure I saw them chatting a few nights ago?'

This was all sounding really forced but it was the best that she could do.

'I don't think Amber knows her that well,' said Jasmine. 'She's never mentioned her to me, so . . .'

She shrugged.

'Oh, right,' Bryony sighed, suddenly aware that she must sound like a right loser talking about a future (non-existent) History project in the middle of the Christmas holidays.

'Never mind. It was just a thought,' said Bryony. 'I mean, History's great and all that but I much prefer, um ... Maths!'

Bryony bit her lip. What was she *doing*? She did like Maths. She liked it a lot. But saying it now wasn't helpful!

'Right then.' Jasmine checked her watch. 'Sorry, but I'd better go. My brother Callum's driving over after work to give me and Amber a lift home. If he remembers, that is,' she added. 'Callum could forget his own birthday!'

Rolling her eyes, Jasmine gave a tut. 'Brothers, eh?'

Bryony nodded, but before she could reply, a snowball came whizzing from Tornado's open door and got her right on the ear. Josh had been helping Finn with Tor, but clearly he'd had enough of that.

'Really funny, Josh!' Bryony called over. Then she turned back to Jasmine.

'Yep – brothers!'

*

After supper Bryony worked on her Friendship Jars. She wasn't needed at tonight's play rehearsal, nor was Josh. But her brother was up in his bedroom reading comics, so it was just Bryony and Mum, which was lovely after all the busyness of the day.

They were in the lounge, the fire was crackling and Mum had a lit a scented candle. Cinnamon and orange. The smell was really dreamy and relaxing.

For Cabbage Patch Charlie's Friendship Jar, Bryony had made some cookies. They were in the shape of radishes, carrots and bees because Charlie loved his allotment. She'd also iced them and put lots of coloured sprinkles on top.

The Coopers' jar was just the right size for the three little picture frames she'd bought from Mr Thimblefold's shop. She hoped they'd soon fill them with happy pictures. Though sadly, she thought, not of Brook Dale . . .

Around the wire handle of each of the jars, Bryony tied a gingham ribbon. Then she polished the outside glass until it sparkled, and attached a label saying who the jar was for, with a little message on the back. The message on Cabbage Patch Charlie's label said:

Grow friends like vegetables!
(Without the watering.)

But the label on the Coopers' was much
more serious:

I'll miss you ...

'They look gorgeous,' said Mum. 'And I know I'm
not really meant to read the labels but I'm sure the
Coopers will miss you too, and remember *you* as a
happy memory of Brook Dale.'

Mum gave her a hug. 'You're really kind. Just
have fun too, and don't take on too much. You
can't always solve everything, eh?'

Bryony nodded. 'I know,' she said quietly. 'If
only ...'

Chapter 12

'A rat! A RAT!' Bryony shrieked.

'Where?' cried Emma.

'There!'

Bryony pointed. 'It just scuttled round the back of that hay bale! All hairy, and ratty – and *massive!*'

It was Thursday morning and the girls were mucking out Piggy in Farmer Jenkins's barn while Red gave a lesson at Seaview.

Emma put down her pitchfork and went to check around the hay bale. Emma wanted to be a vet one day so she didn't mind rats at all.

Bryony did. But she calmed herself quickly so that Piggy didn't get spooked. Not that he looked remotely bothered as he chomped on a mouthful of hay.

'No worries, Bry,' called Emma. 'I think the rat's gone.'

'Oh, good!' Bryony smiled.

But no sooner had she spoken than a thumping filled the air as if Ratty was back — with hobnailed boots on!

Bryony spun around. No rat. Just Jed Jenkins belting up in his big muddy wellies.

'Hey!' gasped Jed, red-faced and panting. 'Have either of you seen Gnawsy?'

'Who's—?' began Bryony.

'My pet rat!' puffed Jed. 'Okay, so there we were in the kitchen 'aving breakfast – me, Goaty, Gnawsy and Fiona.'

'Fiona?' blurted Bryony, glossing over Goaty as *everyone* knew Jed's nightmare pet goat.

'Yeah, Fiona,' nodded Jed. 'She's Gramps's pet pig. And boy, does she love breakfast! Just not *sausages*. Or bacon. *Obviously.*'

Jed was talking like this was a normal thing – having breakfast with a goat, a rat, a pet pig, and the family!

'But then,' went on Jed, 'Gran whips out her trumpet. She's been practising for the play, see?'

Bryony felt herself nod. Though she didn't see at all. This was all kinds of bonkers!

'So anyway, Gran blows her trumpet full-blast. But Gnawsy don't like trumpets, do he?' said Jed.

'D-do he?' repeated Bryony. 'I mean – don't he – err, *doesn't* he?'

'Nah,' tutted Jed. 'He don't!'

Jed shook his head. 'He's sensitive, see. A bit nervy, to be honest, is Gnawsy. So he bolts – *fwittt* – straight out the back door as Gramps is coming in from his gritting. Then Goaty gets all twitchy, 'cos Gnawsy's done a runner. See, Goaty likes Gnawsy. When Gnawsy don't bite him. But Gnawsy only bites 'cos he's *teething*.'

Jed shrugged. 'Anyway, you seen him, then? A cute baby rat – dark grey, kind eyes, sharp(ish) teeth?'

For a moment the girls just stood there, trying to take all this in.

'Um, hay bales,' Emma then muttered quietly.

'Oh, brill!' Jed beamed, clumping over to look, flecks of mud flying off his wellies. A few moments later, he returned looking pleased, with Gnawsy cradled in his arms. Bryony shuddered. It looked like a big fat hairball you'd pull out of the plughole in the bath. Except this one had teeth, and a thick pink swishy tail!

'Here he is!' beamed Jed. 'Cute, eh? Wanna hold?'

'No, thanks!' Bryony squeaked and even Emma politely declined.

'Right then,' said Jed. 'Come on, Gnawsy! He's helping me learn my lines for the play. Cinderella's on my case. She's so stroppy!'

'That doesn't sound like Alice,' Bryony said.

'It ain't Alice no more. It's Georgina now,' said Jed.

'What?' gasped Emma.

'Hang on!' cried Bryony. 'Let me get this straight. Are you saying Georgina Brook is now Cinderella?'

'Yep.'

Jed then told them that at last night's rehearsal Mr Brook had turned up with Georgina.

'So, Mr Brook,' grumbled Jed, 'talked to Pettifour for ages. Then Pettifour asked Alice if she'd be okay to swap, and put *Georgina* as Cinders instead.'

Bryony felt instantly furious for Alice. Georgina *always* got what she wanted!

'So what's Alice now?' Emma asked Jed.

'Um, Ball Crowd,' he nodded. 'And she didn't seem to mind a bit!'

Jed left, and the girls took Piggy to the beach, chattering about the play the whole way there. By the time they arrived, they both agreed that Alice was actually better off with Ball Crowd. Now she'd be with her friends, could forget about the sidecar, and wouldn't have to dance with Jed in those wellies. Now that was all on Georgina – and it served her right!

The beach was deserted and icy cold. The sand was covered in a fresh layer of snow and some of the rock pools had a thin layer of ice at their surface.

The girls took it in turns to ride Piggy. 'I hope his detangle spray works,' said Emma, as she jumped on to have her go. 'You only have to look at his mane and it knots. And we don't have long to get it done now.'

Tomorrow was Christmas Eve and the play was at two o' clock.

'Don't worry,' said Bryony. 'By the time we've finished he'll look gorgeous!'

Piggy gave a snort, sounding thoroughly unimpressed with *that* plan!

Bryony told Emma to ride on. Then stopping, she gave her feet a good stomp to try and get the circulation going. She could hardly feel them. And although it wasn't actually snowing now, the clouds were so high Bryony expected more later.

'Brr!' She shivered, hoping the Coopers were keeping warm. A white Christmas was such a cosy thought. But there were so many things happening before the big day that more snow might well interfere with. How would the postman deliver the Friendship Jars, for instance, if snow blocked all the roads? And constantly keeping Seaview's yard clear was turning into a mammoth operation!

Wrapping her scarf around her, she ran on to catch up with Emma. 'Hey, Em – I'm going to see Meredith after this.'

'Oh, can I come too?' Emma asked. 'I'd love

to meet the family properly after everything you've said.'

'Sure,' Bryony smiled. 'Meredith is going to love Piggy.'

Meredith didn't know that Bryony was coming, but Bryony knew she'd be delighted to see her. Meredith was such a sociable little thing. Though perhaps she'd been a touch subdued when Bryony last visited after the row on the Green. She longed to see Meredith twirl again. Carefree and full of dizzy smiles, like on the first day they'd met.

Bryony was also keen to make the most of the time she and the Coopers still had together. After Tuesday night's argument Mr Cooper had seemed determined to leave town as soon as possible. Then last night, when doing their Friendship Jar, it had struck Bryony that they could go at any moment. She *had* to see Meredith one more time before they left for good.

She still felt determined to solve the case too, although time was rapidly running out. The few disjointed clues that Bryony already had kept whirling around in her head. Hopefully the Coopers would say something today that would give her a bit more of a lead. Although Mr Cooper had told Mr Brook that he knew nothing about the silver, sometimes – or so Miss Swann always said – important clues could just pop out of nowhere.

Mr Thimblefold wasn't doing too well either, which was another reason Bryony couldn't give up. That morning, when Grandpa had appeared with some eggs for breakfast, he'd said that now the sidecar was fixed, Mr Thimblefold was back in his dressing gown and slippers and his beard looked more straggly than ever. His enchanting little shop was still closed too, and whenever Grandpa mentioned it, apparently Mr T just quickly changed the subject.

'Time to get Red, Em,' Bryony nodded. 'He'll definitely have finished his lesson by now and we can ride to the Coopers together.'

'Okay.' Emma turned Piggy around. 'Let's go!'

Bryony walked by their side, still mulling over clues, as Piggy plodded Emma off the beach. Back at Seaview, Bryony left them in the lane and hurried inside to get Red.

'He's really bouncy,' she said, trotting him back out. 'I just told him we were off to see Blossom and he seems so keen.'

Red had a happy spring in his step all the way to the meadow by Bluebell Wood. When they arrived, Mr Cooper was out polishing the huge bear. It appeared to be finished and ready for Saul Salmon a day early.

Bryony bit her lip. Ready a day early? Could the Coopers be leaving *today*? She felt her shoulders sag. Yes, it made sense. They were off.

The girls dismounted by the fir trees and carefully tied up their ponies. Bryony made sure Red was next to Blossom and they greeted each other by blowing noses, just as they'd done the other day. It looked like they'd been friends forever, thought Bryony.

She and Emma walked over to Mr Cooper and as they did so, Bryony saw he looked sad.

'H-how are you doing, Mr Cooper?' she asked.

Mr Cooper stopped polishing. 'Ah, Bryony ... not so great. We've had a visit from the police about the silver.'

'When?' gasped Bryony.

'Yesterday afternoon.'

Mr Cooper, she thought, looked pale and tired, with dark circles under his eyes. Bryony suspected he'd been awake in the night, worrying.

'Aye. Anyway, I told them my story,' he sighed. 'That I just took the sticks from the Brooks' and nothing else. I went through it all, and they listened and wrote things down. But then they told us not to leave for the moment. So it looks like we're around a bit longer.'

'That must have been awful,' Bryony said. Back in her old school in the city, she'd once been 'under suspicion' too when Lara Ford's pencil case had gone missing. She'd had nothing to do with it, and had said so as well. Finally it was found behind some drawers where it had slipped, and Lara had quickly apologised. But Bryony had never forgotten how it felt when she'd simply not been believed . . .

'I believe you, Mr Cooper,' she said. And although she loved having the family around, she longed for them to stay because they *wanted* to, not because they *had* to.

Bryony had quite forgotten Emma standing at her side. 'Oh! This is Emma,' Bryony said, and Mr Cooper gave her a nod.

'Wait, weren't you the girl at the Market?' he asked. 'The one who spoke up with Bryony?'

Emma nodded.

'Well, thank you,' Mr Cooper replied.

Bryony then pointed out Piggy too. He looked like an ant so close to Blossom!

'And Piggy's got the star part in the play,' said Bryony. 'He's going to pull Cinderella's carriage.'

She thought for a moment.

'The play's tomorrow,' she said. 'At two o'clock in the primary school. I know you might not feel like it now, but maybe you could bring Meredith and Morgan? I'm sure Meredith – well, both of them really – would love it.'

Mr Cooper shook his head.

'I'm sure you're right about the twins. But folk wouldn't want, well, you know . . .'

His voice trailed off.

Yes, Bryony *did* know. It was Christmas – a time of caring, and thinking the best of people. Yet, despite all her promises, Brook Dale had let the Coopers down.

The deep heavy silence that seemed to weigh down the air was suddenly broken by the creak of a door and Meredith came running from the caravan.

'Bryony!' she cried. She gave her a huge hug. 'You came. You came to play!'

'Yes,' Bryony nodded, quickly blinking back a tear. 'I came to play anything you – and Morgan – like!'

'Morgan can't,' replied Meredith. 'He's got a tummy ache so he's inside, drawing.'

'Well, you'll have us all to yourself, then!' said Bryony. 'This is Emma. She really wanted to meet you too.'

Meredith smiled at Emma, but as she did, clung on extra tightly to Bryony!

Mrs Cooper now appeared with some of Blossom's old blankets which she kindly used to cover Red and Piggy. As they were stopping for a bit, she said, she wanted to keep the ponies nice and warm.

Bryony and Emma thanked her. Then Meredith announced she was ready to play and reeled off a long list of games.

'Wow!' laughed Bryony. 'That sounds like lots of fun!'

They started with hide-and-seek, which was followed by chase. Then twirling and doing handstands! After that, they played catch and then even tried juggling fir cones.

Finally, they built a snowman and Meredith gave him a lovely bright hat and scarf. Mrs Cooper even brought out a carrot for a nose to finish him.

Although Meredith appeared to like Emma, Bryony was clearly her favourite. Bryony thought this was so cute. Emma had Will to look up to her, and Meredith now felt like the little sister Bryony had never had.

When Emma nipped in to quickly meet Morgan, Bryony gave Meredith a go on Red.

'I want to jump a fence!' Meredith cried. 'That fence by the holly, I *can* jump it!'

'Um . . . maybe next time,' Bryony smiled. 'And maybe a fence not near any prickles, just in case!'

Bryony and Emma stayed for lunch too. They had the most delicious cheese on toast, which they ate inside the cosy caravan. Then Bryony read the twins another chapter of *Alice*. By the time she'd finished, Meredith *certainly* had her sparkle back!

Bryony could hardly bear to leave. 'But I really do have to go now,' she said. 'Red and Piggy need a rest.'

'Oh.' Meredith's little face fell.

'But I'll see you again,' said Bryony. 'Very soon.'

Meredith and Mrs Cooper walked the girls back to the ponies. Then, handing over the blankets, Bryony and Emma jumped on and Bryony gave Meredith a little wave.

'Mum, I *love* Bryony!' Bryony heard her say as Red trotted off through the snow.

'Oh, Em!' gasped Bryony. 'Did you hear that?!'

'So sweet!' replied Emma. 'But . . .'

'What?' asked Bryony.

'Well, maybe try not to get too attached. Because, you know . . . they'll be leaving.'

And Bryony suddenly heard herself whisper, 'Too late.'

*

'Hello, girls!' said Hari's mum as she let Bryony and Emma inside.

'Hi!' said Bryony, and Emma nodded back with a smile.

Hari's house was very tall and made from red bricks. Bryony thought it was ever so pretty. It had a lilac front door and a porch with panels of square-shaped stained glass in pinks, greens, yellows and light blues.

The Super Six were meeting here to get their costumes ready for the play. The girls were accessorising some beautiful dresses they were borrowing off Hari's older sisters, and Josh and Finn were going to make some sashes for their Ball suits.

'Looking forward to the play, then?' Hari's mum asked, now leading them down the narrow hallway.

'Yes!' replied Emma.

'Me too,' said Bryony. 'So much!'

Hari's mum nodded. 'Not much longer to wait. Better get those ball gowns finished! Harita and the others are already in the craft den, you know the way.'

Hari's mum, who was also one of the town doctors, sewed quilts in her spare time, so had converted the garden shed into a cool crafting workshop.

'Thanks,' said the girls, heading through the kitchen and out of the back door on the other side. A set of garden steps led to a narrow path down to the bottom of the garden. Everything was covered in thick snow, including Hari's big trampoline on the lawn.

They followed the path to a little wooden shed with pots of winter violas on the windowsills. Today, in the snow, it reminded Bryony of a ski lodge and Georgina suddenly crossed her mind. Huh! She *was* going skiing after all. Yet again her scheming had paid off.

Bryony quickly brushed the thought away. Mum had told her she must have more fun, and that having a break at Hari's would help her think more clearly about the mystery. She was determined, then, to really enjoy this afternoon!

'Come on, Em.' Bryony opened the shed door and they hurried in to see the others.

'Wow!' she gasped.

'Ooo!' cried Emma. 'Amazing!'

It looked like a rainbow had exploded in there. There were dresses of every colour! Pink, yellow, green, blue, orange, purple – and the brightest red. Bryony really didn't know where to start!

'Come and pick!' Hari called. 'Look! There are tons to choose from!'

'I'm having this turquoise one!' Alice beamed.

'Lovely!' smiled Bryony, thrilled to see that Alice seemed genuinely happy to be in the Ball Crowd. And in *these* dresses, Bryony thought, the Ball Crowd would *seriously* sparkle!

Josh and Finn needed bright sashes and cummerbunds too. They'd be wearing suits but Mr Pettifour had instructed them to add 'a pop of colour'.

'Hmm, *orange* for me, I think,' said Josh.

'And could Will have some too?' Emma asked. 'I need to make him a pumpkin costume.'

'Sure!' Hari nodded. 'And Mum's got tons of cushions to pad him out with.'

Bryony chose her dress and it was great fun sewing on sequins, beads, and lace, and making flowers out of felt and ribbons!

It turned out that Finn was fantastic at 'accessorising'. He'd read books on it (surprise, surprise!). By the time they'd finished, they all had a costume they were proud of.

Emma's gown was emerald green, Alice had her turquoise, Hari had wanted something really zingy so had chosen a shocking pink, Finn's sash and cummerbund were purple, and Josh had gone for scarlet in the end, to kindly save all the orange fabric for Will's pumpkin costume.

As for Bryony, her gown was silvery-blue. She'd also stitched on some shiny lime-green sequins which sparkled like real jewels.

They even made a feathery plume hat for Piggy which they'd clip in his long shaggy mane.

'But I'm not sure,' said Emma, 'you'll even be able to see it. His hair still looks like candyfloss!'

'*Fear not!*' cried Bryony in an-over-the-top voice and bowing low like a medieval lord. '*For it shall be decreed, that tomorrow morn, Seaview Stables shall becometh a Piggy Pamper Parlour! And his impossible locks shall again be detangled. And he shall really looketh the part!*'

Alice kindly offered to lend a hand too and Emma and Bryony were so grateful.

'I could even braid him!' said Alice enthusiastically.

That night the play's dress rehearsal went quite well. Jed was still in his (not allowed!) wellies, but treading on *Georgina's* toes instead of Alice's now. Georgina was fuming, which made it all the more entertaining!

The two Miss Ps were still squabbling too, but that was to be expected. Tonight it was over who had the *highest* hairdo. Both, apparently, had spent hours at the hairdresser's – and were threatening to go back!

'You wait till tomorrow afternoon,' snapped Miss Pigeon. 'My bun will be EVEN higher!'

'Huh! Mine too!' Miss Parsley boomed. 'With BOWS in!!'

Bryony knew she'd have to sort her own hair out too. Never a happy thought. If only there was the equivalent of a mane-detangling spray for people with impossible curls! She quickly consoled herself with the happy thought that her ball gown, at least, was impeccable. Plus, she and her friends easily had the best 'pop of colour' costumes in the room!

'Well, *darlings!*' twinkled Mr Pettifour at the end. 'We're getting somewhere *finally*, aren't we? Now, keep practising those lines. Jed – no wellies tomorrow. And please arrive *promptly* at one o'clock which will give us an hour to do make-up and hair before it's "Showtime!" at two!'

He dismissed them with a dramatic wave of the arm. 'And get lots of beauty sleep tonight!'

'I hope you're not looking at *me*?' scowled Miss Pigeon.

'Or me!' yelled Miss Parsley, and Mr Pettifour swallowed hard.

'O-of course not!'

Bryony walked home with Emma, who was staying with her for a sleepover. After a steaming hot fish pie for supper, the girls retreated to Bryony's bedroom.

As the Coopers' moon gazing hare had been sold, Bryony had decided to knit Mum a Christmas scarf. Bryony loved her own scarf so much and hoped the one she'd knit for Mum would become *her* favourite too. Yesterday she'd spent the last of her pocket money on buying lots of balls of wool, and she had started the scarf late last night after the Friendship Jars. She still had loads to knit though, and it *wasn't* going well.

'Oh, no,' sighed Bryony, dropping yet another stitch. That was hole number eight right there.

'But at least,' said Bryony, 'it'll be made with *tons of love*. And that's the main thing, right?'

Emma smiled back with an encouraging thumbs up.

'Yeah,' nodded Bryony.

'Made with tons of love . . .' She'd make sure to write that on the label!

Chapter 13

Bryony had been right about those high clouds yesterday. When she peeped through her curtains on Christmas Eve morning, small fluffy snowflakes were drifting from the sky and making the garden look simply magical.

'Oh, Em. I do love this place!' she cried as a robin bobbed along her windowsill.

'Let's go and have breakfast. And then,' smiled Bryony, 'it's Piggy pamper-time and the play!'

Emma's jaw dropped. 'Piggy. I'd forgotten. What if he doesn't *detangle*?'

'He will,' nodded Bryony grabbing the spray. 'Between this, and Alice's expert braiding, he'll look great!'

The girls got washed and dressed at breakneck speed. Quickly folding the scarf she'd now finished for Mum, Bryony hid it under her pillow. It was a little bit wonky and had eleven holes now. But Bryony did have some very pretty wrapping paper and, as well as writing the tons of love bit, she also planned to decorate the label!

The girls followed the dreamy smell of breakfast downstairs. Grandpa was in the kitchen cooking bacon and eggs. Bryony remembered he'd come over early to pick up some garlands Mum had made to decorate Cinderella's sidecar.

'Hi, Gramps!' cried Bryony.

'Hello, girls,' he smiled back. 'Right, who's hungry, then?'

'I am!' called Josh, already at the table, and Bryony and Emma both nodded and went to join him.

As they sat down Mum came over with some apple juice.

'Sleep well?' she asked.

'I did,' nodded Emma.

'Me too – eventually,' Bryony said. 'I was doing . . . something until quite late. But no asking!'

Breakfast was delicious. It was just what they needed to set them up for the day.

'And can we have the same tomorrow?' asked Josh. Grandpa would be spending Christmas Day with them.

Tomorrow! thought Bryony. It was Christmas Day *tomorrow*. She couldn't wait!

'Of course you can, Josh.' Grandpa grinned. His bacon and eggs with all the trimmings was becoming a Christmas tradition. Bryony liked that. Making traditions. Like they used to have back in the city. They were different ones here. But that was okay. She was learning that 'different', like a new pony, just needed time to settle in.

Tomorrow after breakfast, Bryony would *insist* they opened their stockings by the fire. Then right after that she'd pop along to Seaview to wish Red a happy Christmas too. When she got back, they'd exchange family presents and soon there'd be wrapping paper everywhere! Josh would most likely plant a gift bow on Berry's head because some things never change. The cat would swipe it off and grumpily march away to strop under the Christmas tree!

Bryony smiled. Making memories really helped

her feel part of Brook Dale. But she felt her smile start to fade as she thought of the Coopers again. How out of place they must feel here now. And they couldn't even leave . . .

For them, and kind old Mr Thimblefold, Christmas would dawn under a cloud of worry as heavy as the snow clouds above town. *Unless*, thought Bryony, she could solve the case. Solve the case and prove them innocent!

But how? Now that Christmas Eve was here, she was fighting a battle against time. Between ponies, plays, Friendship Jars and carol singing – when would there be time for hunting out more clues? Or mulling over the few they already had? She had to keep thinking!

After breakfast the girls needed to go and see Red and Piggy. They were gathering their things when they were stopped in their tracks by a hurried knock at the door.

Bryony opened it.

'Hi, Bry!' whispered Finn. 'I've got news!' Bryony quickly invited him in. Mum and Grandpa were busy in the lounge so the children had the kitchen to themselves.

'What is it?' asked Josh.

'You okay?' Emma asked.

'Yeah,' replied Finn. 'It's about the case.'

Bryony gasped, '*You found something out?*' and Finn nodded.

'Remember on Mr Brook's notepad,' he said, 'you saw the word LAPADA?'

'Yes!'

'So, LAPADA,' went on Finn, 'actually stands for London And Provincial Antique Dealers' Association. Bry, Cuthbert and Fig – the names you saw on the box – they're antique dealers! They polish and restore things made from silver too.'

'Hey, Finn, how come you know this?' asked Josh. He looked really impressed.

'I told my dad what we'd already found out,' said Finn, 'and we did a bit of searching on his laptop last night.'

'Hang on!' said Bryony. 'Cuthbert and Fig *polish* and *restore* things, you said?'

Finn grinned. 'The penny's just dropped, hasn't it?'

'Yes!' cried Bryony.

'Not for me . . .' frowned Josh, and Emma also looked blank.

199

'Those other letters on Mr Brook's notepad!' replied Bryony. 'P and R – they stand for Polish and Restore!'

'Restore?' asked Emma.

'It means repair,' answered Bryony.

'It sure does!' said Finn. 'Cuthbert and Fig have a shop on Pudding Lane. Me and Dad street-viewed it on the laptop. Really swish!'

'Finn, you're a genius!' Bryony beamed. 'Listen, me and Em have to go now but we'll pick this up again as soon as we can.'

'Okay!' nodded Finn. 'I'll go fill in the others.'

'Good plan!

Finn left, and as Bryony gathered up her riding things, her brain was working nineteen-to-the-dozen. At last they were starting to get somewhere with the case. But still her thoughts were in a bit of a jumble.

As the silver was now being cleaned – or restored – could *this* be some sort of clue? She couldn't see how. But maybe she just needed more time ...

Then there were those passers-by Mr Thimblefold had glimpsed just moments after the silver had been dumped in his shop. The lady with the brown furry headband. The man with the beanie hat and ginger hair. And those penguins! Suspects? Or just random people on their way home?

'Come on, Em,' said Bryony. She'd let her brain mull all this over as the day unfolded.

'Ready!' smiled Emma, zipping up her coat.

'Oh, wait!' said Mum, reappearing with Grandpa. 'Take these too.' She took two brown paper bags from the fridge and gave the girls one each.

'Sandwiches, in case you don't make it back for lunch,' Mum said.

They thanked her and decided to take their costumes for the play too. Bryony also got her Friendship Jars. These had to be left in a classroom in school to be collected by the postman after the play. Emma's dad was going to drop hers off.

The girls headed out. It was a beautiful morning! The sun was shining through the snowflakes and everything was twinkly and bright.

The pond down the lane was completely iced over and now a skating rink for ducks. And the happy little things were having the time of their lives!

'Quack! Quack!' They slipped and slid and

whirled. To Bryony, it sounded as if they were calling a noisy, 'Merry Christmas!'

Further on, as the girls approached Seaview, they saw the Stormy Point Lighthouse on the tip of the headland. The overnight snow had gathered on its top and frozen in a tall fluffy peak.

'Oh, Em!' Bryony pointed. 'Lookout Towers is wearing a bobble hat!'

Seaview looked busy with riders coming and going. Amber Stepney came out on Dash and Jess on Destiny behind her.

'Tons happening today, Bry!' Jess called to Bryony.

'I know,' nodded Bryony. 'Can't wait!'

At the stable gate Bryony turned to Emma who was about to head on to White Mouse Farm.

'Em, fancy a quick gallop before pamper-time?' she asked. 'We could meet at the beach at nine thirty?'

'Sounds like a plan,' Emma smiled back. 'See you there!'

With a wave, Bryony went in through the gate, the snow squeaking under her boots. The Christmas tree was lit. But the clear plastic bauble with Red's picture in was no longer at the top. It seemed Tiberius had now taken top spot!

'Huh!' Bryony couldn't help but laugh. Some mischievous elf must have switched them in the night. (Tabby's mum!)

She hurried on to the yard. Red's top door was open and there he was, peeping out.

'Happy Christmas Eve!' Bryony cried. His ears perked up and his eyes twinkled as he let out the happiest of nickers.

'Yes, I know!' Bryony giggled. 'It's so exciting!'

She stroked his muzzle and he nudged her hand, his little kiss curl bouncing. Tomorrow, thought Bryony, he'd love his new play ball. She was going to wrap it too. She was bursting to tell him but that would spoil the surprise, so she resisted being a chatterbox for once.

Opening the stable door, she went inside and quickly began her chores. When Red had had breakfast and a nice fresh drink, it was time to get on with the mucking out. She was always very thorough when it came to keeping his stable clean, but she wanted it to be extra spick and span when Christmas Day dawned.

Bryony led him out to the turnout paddock to have some exercise while she did this. There were a few other ponies there too, including Daffy and Princess P.

Returning to the stable with a wheelbarrow, Bryony began by forking out Red's droppings, then the wet patches of sawdust.

Each time she got a wheelbarrow full she had to take it round to the heap. Today this was taking slightly longer because she had to make sure she didn't slip in the snow.

'Right!' said Bryony, now adding fresh sawdust to the clean stuff she'd left on Red's floor. She fluffed it with a pitchfork as she went, and did the same when adding clean straw. This she then banked up along the walls to stop any nasty draughts. And finally, after a quick brush around, she brought Red back in to groom him.

'Isn't your stable smart?' said Bryony. 'And later tonight, if you hear any hooves tippy-tapping across your roof, you know who it'll be, don't you, eh?'

Red nuzzled her playfully, his dark eyes twinkling.

'That's right!' nodded Bryony. 'Santa's

reindeers – that's who. And do make sure that you tell them where Plum Cottage is!'

Bryony brushed Red down and rubbed oil into his hooves. Then she checked his tack. His saddle looked a bit dusty so she cleaned it with saddle soap and finished off with conditioner to add shine. Just a little, though, so it wouldn't be too slippery when she rode him.

'Good boy, Red,' said Bryony as she tacked him up. He was standing really still. 'Now I just need to check you over. Let's see . . .'

Red's bit looked comfy and in the right position, his noseband and throatlatch weren't too loose or too tight, and the reins were fastened properly.

His saddle looked nice and comfy too. The pads were straight, the girth straps weren't twisted and the buckles were all correctly positioned with none pressing into Red's skin.

'You are an absolute picture!' Bryony said.

She quickly jumped on and off they went, meeting Emma and Piggy at the beach right on time. With a brisk sea breeze flying through his mane as he galloped along the sand, Red felt like he could happily exercise for hours.

Piggy, as ever, really struggled to keep up. But he was trying so hard today. In the end Bryony had to rein Red in a little, mindful not to push Piggy too hard or he'd be reluctant to move later in the play!

After a brisk gallop, they returned to Seaview where Red went in for a rest. Bryony then joined Emma, Alice and Piggy in a spare stable that Abi had said they could use to get Piggy ready for the play.

'Ready to detangle then?' Alice asked with a smile.

'As ready as I'll ever be!' gulped Emma.

First they gave Piggy's mane and tail a quick sponge down. Then, using a fresh tack-cleaning sponge, they massaged the detangler into his tangles and finger-combed it, starting at the bottom and working upwards.

Piggy didn't seem to mind this at all, and with three of them it was much faster than Emma doing it alone. When his mane and tail looked nice and shiny, they gave them a little shampoo to get rid of any traces of detangler. Finally, when it was dry and carefully brushed, Alice took over French-braiding Piggy's mane. By the time she'd finished you could hardly recognise him.

'Oh, Piggy!' beamed Emma. 'You'll look even prettier than Cinderella!'

Bryony checked her watch. It was half past twelve. They had to be at the school hall in half an hour so it was almost time to head off. It usually took about eight or so minutes to walk to town from the stables but it was bound to take longer in the snow.

After wolfing down their sandwiches, the girls hurried to the gate. The others were waiting, and as they walked to town, Finn filled them in on Cuthbert and Fig.

'Hooray! We're *getting* somewhere!' Alice cried.

'Yeah, we are,' Bryony nodded. She still had no answers, but discussing theories felt somehow very useful.

The closer they got to her old school, the more excited Bryony became about the play. The entire town seemed to be out doing last-minute things before it started. Some were bustling about getting last-minute Christmas presents, while others picked up turkeys or cakes. Fresh snow was being shovelled from pathways and steps. And the postman was only just making it around town delivering the final cards and parcels before the big day.

Children were absolutely everywhere too – building snowmen, throwing snowballs, or whooshing along on sledges. Miss Pigeon had closed the post office early and was back in the hairdresser's again. Bryony saw her with a head full of curlers.

'Huh! Miss Parsley won't be happy about that!' grinned Bryony.

Hurrying on, they turned up Chestnut Lane where they bumped into Farmer Jenkins who was sitting in his tractor.

'Gritting again?' called up Bryony. But the farmer shook his head.

'Nah, me bloomin' tractor's just broke!'

'Oh, no!' gasped Bryony, and she whispered to Josh, 'He'll be totally lost without his gritting.'

'And for once,' replied Josh under his breath, 'it actually needs doing!'

As they shuffled in through the snowy school gates, a group of helpers were getting things ready. Some were clearing the car park, while others put up lights and a tree.

The Friendship Jars had to be left in the Year Six classroom. 'Best do that first,' Bryony said. Some of the others had their jars too.

As she stepped back into her old classroom, it felt odd, but in a good way. And the Friendship Jars looked so pretty all gathered together.

The children peeped inside them and read the tags, which all had different messages on. Some even had pictures – reindeers, and trees, and Bryony spotted one of a cat waving a pirate flag!

When the postman collected them after the play he'd be surprised to see a new address too ...

The Cooper Family.
The Caravan,
Near the Holly Bush,
Bluebell Wood

Next they went to check out the hall. 'Ooo!' cried Bryony. 'The stage looks great!'

Mr Pettifour was up there with his 'set-painting party' giving Cinderella's village backdrop its final dabs of paint.

Bryony also spied one of Mr Thimblefold's

beautiful clocks for when the clock struck midnight at the Ball scene later.

'Hey, there's Gramps!' said Josh and Bryony waved.

'Oh, and look!'

Helping Grandpa decorate the sidecar with flowers was Mr Thimblefold! She didn't know *how* Gramps had managed to do that, but was thrilled to see Mr T out and about again.

The infant classrooms had been set up as dressing rooms. Bryony and the others checked each of them out to see which had most space – and it was like peeping into very busy fairy tales!

There were swarms of little children dressed as white mice in fluffy dressing gowns with crepe paper ears. They were whooping and shrieking as they chased about, trying to pull off each other's tails. Bryony then heard one being 'spoken to' by her mum . . .

'Cinderella's mice were all *sensible*, Eloise – so please calm down.'

There were one or two Village Crowd wandering about too, and lots of Ball Crowd getting ready for the Palace. The back end of a cow (Saul Salmon, the fishmonger) had lost its front end (Cabbage Patch Charlie), and there were footmen and trumpeters (including Jed's gran!), and a very smart coachman in a red and gold tailcoat, called Rory.

Bryony then saw the rat (Henry Pringle) who, in the original fairy tale, '*magically transformed*' into the very smart coachman in the red and gold tailcoat. Henry Pringle was wearing a dark grey leotard, pink tights and a very big scowl.

As he obviously couldn't be '*magically transformed*' into the coachman on stage, when Fairy Godmother tapped Henry with her wand, his stage direction was to 'Belt off left – fast' so that Rory, the coachman in the red and gold tailcoat, could be 'Shoved *on* left – fast'. Fingers crossed, thought Bryony, both boys knew their 'left' from their 'right'!

Henry did not look happy to be there. His mum said he was 'totally over' his recent bout of chickenpox, but Bryony wasn't so sure. Even plastered in stage make-up, Henry's blisters still looked weepy. Like volcanoes about to erupt. Plus, he was crying. And scratching. (An awful lot.)

All the costumes looked great as people fussed,

smoothed and pinned them. Tabby made a wonderfully evil Wicked Stepmother in a no-nonsense jacket and bustled skirt, Miss Lightfoot (Fairy Godmother) wore a lilac ballet tutu, and Jed Jenkins was pulling out all the stops, giving his wellies a quick spit and polish.

The Miss Ps, however, easily took the prize for the most over-the-top hairdos. They could hardly stand straight, their buns were so high as they teetered about practising their lines ...

'Tie my dress!'

'Fetch my comb!'

'I is prettier than *you*.'

'NO YOU AIN'T!'

Bryony and her friends slipped into their own costumes and helped Will into his pumpkin suit. It was clear that Emma had used a bit too much padding because Will was getting wedged in doors. But Josh soon came up with a technical solution.

'What?' asked Bryony.

'Squeeze him.'

The Super Six now took themselves off to a quiet corridor to run through their tricky Ball dances, and were right in the middle of a Viennese Waltz when . . .

'Miaaowwww!'

Bryony stopped in mid-spin. It was Blueberry Muffin. Mum had brought him up in his carry-case. The sweet smell of roses suddenly wafted through the air. Clearly Mum had bathed him for the Ball!

'How's Stepmother's cat then?' Bryony asked.

'Disgustingly grouchy,' Mum replied.

'Completely in role then!' Bryony beamed. 'Well done, Berry!'

'But never mind the cat,' said Mum. 'I have a bit of bad news.'

'What?' cried Bryony, and the others gathered round.

'Well, Piggy's arrived,' Mum went on. 'But no one, it appears, thought how to attach the sidecar. Abi's not sure. They've tried – but nothing's working. So Mr Pettifour has said that Piggy can't go on. And Cinderella will have to *walk* to the Ball!'

'Oh dear!' Emma gasped. 'Now everyone will blame Piggy!'

'Wait, don't worry, Em!' Bryony cried. 'There

213

must be *something* we can do.' She wracked her brains. 'Oh! *I'll* pull the sidecar!'

Everyone looked dumbstruck.

'No – listen,' said Bryony. 'I'll crouch down round the side of Piggy so that the audience won't see. Then *I'll* pull the sidecar but they'll all think it's Piggy!'

Emma looked petrified, and Bryony felt a bit nervous. But the show had to go on! So, grabbing Emma's arm, Bryony dragged her off to pitch the idea to Mr Pettifour.

They found him on the field, still with Abi and Piggy, and Bryony delivered her solution.

When she'd finished it was Mr Pettifour's turn to look dumbstruck.

'Trust me!' said Bryony.

'Piggy does,' added Abi.

'And we can't have Cinderella *walking* to the Ball,' chipped in Emma.

Mr Pettifour flicked his fringe, thinking. He wasn't happy but finally agreed. He flounced back in and a beaming Abi followed as she needed to get a seat. It was a quarter to two and the doors were about to open to the public.

On the snowy lane the audience were arriving in droves. Most people were crunching up on foot. But one or two cars had just about made it up to the car park beside the school.

To her delight, Bryony then saw the Coopers coming along in their caravan. Blossom was making very light work of all the snow!

'Hello!' called Bryony. She waved but they didn't see. She hadn't expected them to come, but was thrilled that they had. They deserved to be here as much as anyone else!

'Ah! Here you are.' Georgina Brook now swanned out in a beautiful pink silk dress. She was meant to be in rags for the opening scenes but had refused to wear anything that looked 'tatty'.

'Get that dozy pony in, we're about to start!' she snapped. 'And he better not mess up – *or else.*'

'He won't!' frowned Bryony but Georgina just marched off. Then Bryony turned to Piggy.

'We can *do* this, Piggy,' she said with a nod. 'Just follow my lead, okay?'

'And please don't poop on stage!' added Emma nervously.

Piggy blinked back, as laid-back as ever, but who knew what he'd be like in the spotlight.

'Good luck, guys!' came a friendly voice, and Bryony turned to see Jasmine Stepney heading in with her sister, Amber.

'Just in time!' Bryony called.

'You're telling me,' puffed Jasmine. She nodded to the car park behind her where a van – with a model of a big tap on its roof – was being redirected into a better space.

'It's Callum's,' called Jasmine. 'My brother – he's a plumber. Right *drip*, if you ask me, too. We told him to set off earlier but does he ever listen?'

She stomped the snow off her boots, then she and Amber went inside to get seats.

'Time to get Piggy in too,' said Bryony. 'He *can't* be late to the Ball!'

Chapter 14

It was going so well. So very well. No tears from Tabby, no wedged moments from the pumpkin, no stropping from the VERY Beautiful Sisters.

The audience were loving it, *oooing* and *booing* in all the right places. And Berry was being a right little grump-bag – tick!

Piggy looked just the part too. Waiting patiently in the wings with Bryony, he was *even* hitched up to the sidecar. Mr Cooper had kindly helped attach it, used to getting Blossom on and off the caravan all the time. *Dare* Bryony think it – but this play was turning into a triumph!

In a sudden flourish of tinkly music, Fairy Godmother then twirled onto the stage. It was time for Cinderella to get her beautiful ball gown, for Will pumpkin to transform into a carriage (well, sidecar), and for Henry the rat to 'Belt off left – fast' to be replaced by Rory the smart coachman.

All the little white mice (headed by chief mouse, Eloise) were waiting in the wings to go on. Will was growing nicely in Cinderella's garden, and Henry Pringle was standing beside Bryony in the wings, picking a scab, and grizzling.

Georgina Brook was up on stage and Blueberry Muffin was sat at her feet looking grumpy.

Bryony listened as Georgina discovered Fairy Godmother tiptoeing along through the pumpkin patch. Georgina was word-perfect as she delivered her lines. Actually, thought Bryony, she was doing a really good job.

Fairy Godmother then asked her to find a pumpkin, which she did. Then a couple of small white mice.

'Go on!' Bryony gave Eloise's gang the nod and they scampered out onto the stage looking cute. They had pony ears to wear later on when they'd transform into Piggy's assistant ponies. Bryony had never been sure about this. It was going to be very 'busy' on stage. But Mr Pettifour had said it would add to the 'dramatic effect'.

Bryony now turned to get Henry Pringle set.

'Hang on,' she said.

Where had he gone?

Then she spotted him further back down the wings, talking to Jed Jenkins (and still scratching a scab).

'Psst! Henry!' whispered Bryony. 'You're on in a sec, come back up here now!'

But Henry shook his head.

'Shan't!' he called back. 'I'm poorly and *I'm not going to do it!*'

Bryony froze. There *had* to be a rat. The rat who turned into the coachman!

'Henry,' hissed Bryony. But Henry stomped off and Jed came clumping up instead.

'Listen, don't worry,' Jed whispered with a nod. 'I knew Henry was poorly – so earlier on I sent Gramps back up to the farm. He had to *walk* it of course, 'cos his tractor's bust, but . . .'

'Jed!' whispered Bryony, her head starting to spin. 'Why?'

And then she saw it. A fat hairy *rat's* tail dangling down out of Prince Charming's pocket!

'J-Jed, you *haven't*,' spluttered Bryony. 'Your gramps didn't bring . . . *thingy*?!'

'Gnawsy! Yep, sure did!' beamed Jed. 'I knew Henry would bail so Gnawsy's all set to save the play!'

Jed plunged his hand into his jacket pocket and scooped out the massive grey rat. It was gnawing at, what looked like, a giant chocolate button.

Piggy, who was standing beside Bryony, luckily hadn't seen the rat. Bryony needed to keep it that way too. Who *knew* what Piggy would do if he actually did!

'Jed – no!' whispered Bryony. 'You *absolutely* cannot put that rat on stage.'

Jed grinned. 'You worry too much, you do. He's a cute pet rat, not a dinosaur.' And placing Gnawsy down on the floor, 'Go find Cinderella!' he said.

Bryony *so* wanted to do something, but it was like she was in a trance. The *actor* rat had chickenpox, so the *real* rat (who ate chocolate buttons?) was about to make his stage debut. Really! This could *only* happen in Brook Dale!

She swallowed hard. 'Jed, *no*,' she pleaded. But

the rat was already away! Bryony could see his fat pink tail whipping the floor as he scurried out into the spotlight.

The rest was a blur. A horrible blur. Fairy Godmother screamed. The audience gasped. And Bryony bolted onto the stage.

'Gnawsy – come back here!' she cried. But Gnawsy was not inclined to listen. He was running about left, right and centre – *loving it*!

Fairy Godmother promptly scarpered, as did all the white mice. Georgina, *furious* that Bryony had appeared, now marched away to strop in the pumpkin patch as Will bounded over to try and help Bryony catch Gnawsy.

Bryony looked around.

'But where IS the rat?' she cried. She couldn't see him anywhere.

'Left!' roared the audience.

'Left . . . left . . . right!'

'HE'S BEHIND YOU!!'

Suddenly there was an ear-splitting shriek and Bryony looked behind her. Gnawsy was dangling from the hem of Georgina's dress.

'Argghhhhh!!'

Georgina was properly pink in the face. She peered through the spotlights seeking out her parents, who were sitting in the front row (naturally).

'Daddy!' shrieked Georgina. 'It's chewing my dress!'

'We're coming, Georgie darling!' Her parents leaped off their seats and hurried towards the stage.

In a whim Georgina started spinning around, trying to whoosh off the rat. Bryony and Will began dashing round after her.

'Stop!' yelled Bryony.

'Yeah, Cinders.' Jed marched up. 'You'll make him sick with all that spinning!'

'Never mind *him*!' Georgina shrieked back. 'This is meant to be *my* moment! How *dare* he muscle in! I'm *meant* to be getting my ball gown!'

Georgina's parents were now up on stage too and getting in the way. Then Bryony suddenly saw a spinning grey hairball fly through the air into the audience. Georgina had done it. She'd managed to fling Gnawsy off!

'But *look*, Bry!' cried Will. The cat had seen it too and had sprung off the stage in pursuit.

'He'd better not eat Gnawsy!' Jed glowered at Bryony.

'Well, *catch* your rat then,' Bryony hissed back, 'before Berry does!'

The audience had now turned decidedly twitchy.

'Eeeekkkk!' shrieked a teenager in the front row. She leaped up and her popcorn flew everywhere.

Bryony jumped off the stage, Jed hot on her heels, while Georgina fumed to her parents.

'Daddy! Make them start that scene again!'

'Pettifour! Where are you?!' Mr Brook bellowed. 'This play is turning into a JOKE!'

But it would be no joke, Bryony thought, if Berry *did* catch Gnawsy. Although she didn't exactly like Jed's 'pet', she couldn't bear the thought of anything bad happening to *anything*.

People were flapping and fidgeting now. A group of small children had started to scream and one couple were even standing on their chairs! This, thought Bryony, was all getting way out of hand.

Blueberry wasn't giving up either. As Bryony searched for the rat, on hands and knees, she occasionally caught sight of a fluffy grey tail as her cat did *exactly* the same!

And then she saw it: a fat pink tail whipping

about like a great monster worm! Bryony froze mid-crawl.

'Gnawsy ...' she gulped under her breath. He was three rows from the front, and a couple of seats in, sitting on a hat on the floor. There were several pairs of feet around him but he was definitely within diving-for distance. If Bryony dared ...

She swallowed hard. Catch Gnawsy now and it wasn't too late to finish the play. The play the entire town had worked so hard on. But she didn't like rats. She'd never liked rats. They made her go all wobbly.

Gnawsy's back was to her and he was panting for breath. He hadn't seen her, which was good. She had to keep it like that or he'd be off again.

Taking a deep, calming breath, Bryony knew it was all down to her. So, counting to three in her head – *she dived for him!*

As she flew through the air Bryony really hoped that the rat wouldn't *gnaw* her when caught. But he was called 'Gnawsy' after all, so the clue – very probably – was in the name.

Suddenly she was there. There was no going back. And her fingers closed around his body. She *had* him. Gnawsy was firmly in her grip. She'd done it!

Then it dawned on her that she *did* have him. 'Ewww!' Bryony shuddered. He was plump, and very hairy. And that *tail*!

She waited for the nip. But it didn't come. Then Gnawsy turned and gazed up at her with big round twinkly eyes. He looked petrified and quite worn out. His whiskers were rippling, his small nose twitching nervously, and she could feel the pump, pump, pump of his little beating heart.

Bryony realised now that she'd judged him too soon. *Everyone* deserved a fair chance after all. Even rats.

Gnawsy blinked and took a small shuddering breath.

'It's okay,' whispered Bryony. 'I won't hurt you.' Actually he was quite all right, she thought. Even cute.

She now realised that she was still on the floor. Still flat on her tummy across several pairs of feet. She glanced up, to see the owners of the feet looking down at her.

'Hi, Bry,' muttered Jasmine Stepney. And Amber and their brother, Callum, gave her a little nod.

'Oh, yeah,' Bryony nodded back. 'Err . . . hi.'

225

She quickly shuffled backwards out of the row, carefully holding Gnawsy, who seemed content. It was like he, sort of, knew she'd saved him from Berry.

'Sorry about that,' Bryony said to the Stepneys.

'No worries!' Jasmine now grinned back. 'But maybe return the *massive* rat to its owner?'

'Yeah – right!'

Bryony went to head off. But as she did, the hat on the floor that Gnawsy had been sitting on suddenly caught her eye again.

It was a beanie hat.

Bryony stopped.

Then her gaze slowly drifted to its owner ... Jasmine's brother.

'You okay, Bry?' asked Jasmine.

'Ginger hair,' mumbled Bryony. 'Beanie hat and ... bright ginger hair.'

She pointed at Callum Stepney.

'Um, yeah,' Jasmine nodded. 'The whole family have ginger hair, what's wrong with that?'

'No, n–nothing!' Bryony heard herself say as her brain began whirring again.

There was something very important about

what she'd just discovered. But Bryony wasn't sure what – yet . . .

When the audience had settled, the play resumed. But Bryony couldn't stop thinking about ginger hair.

Ginger hair, ginger hair – all through the Ball.

Ginger hair, as the clock struck midnight.

Cinderella ran. The Prince found her glass slipper . . .

Ginger hair, ginger hair, ginger hair.

And then, in the wedding scene, as Piggy pulled the carriage away, 'Ginger hair!' cried Bryony, pointing from the stage to Callum Stepney.

Suddenly she felt her cheeks go hot. She *so* wasn't one for sudden outbursts like this but she had to go along with it now.

Besides, she'd done it! She had *finally* solved 'The Mystery of the Silver'. (At least she *hoped* she had, or this was going to be embarrassing.)

'Um, Callum,' called Bryony, waving a ball-gowned arm and making her way downstage. She stopped at the front, finding herself in the spotlight, and heard a tutting Georgina behind.

'So, Callum,' continued Bryony, shielding her eyes with her hand, 'you're a plumber, aren't you? I mean – outside,' she said, 'I just saw the office van with the tap on?'

Callum nodded uncertainly. 'Yeah,' he called back. 'But I am allowed to borrow the van. My boss don't mind if I'm careful.'

'No, what I was getting at,' Bryony went on, 'was ... did *your* plumbing company fix the Brooks' toilets?'

'Excuse *me*!' cried Mr Brook. He jumped up from his seat and the audience started tittering. A frenzied Mr Pettifour then hurried out on stage. He snapped his twinkly clapperboard.

'CUT!'

'No! Let her speak – and 'im as well!' snapped Miss Pigeon, pointing from the stage to Callum.

Callum swallowed hard, then looked back at Bryony. 'Well, um ... yeah,' he replied. 'We did fix the Brooks' toilets. Why?'

'So ...' But Bryony stopped, feeling every pair of eyes in the entire room on her face.

'You can do it,' Emma whispered. All her friends had gathered round.

'Just trust your instinct,' whispered Finn.

'Yeah,' nodded Josh. 'You're so smart.'

Bryony cleared her throat.

'S-so, Callum,' she said. 'If it's okay, would you mind putting on your beanie hat, please?'

'Err ...' said Callum. He gave a puzzled shrug. 'Um, I suppose.'

As he did, Bryony walked down the steps to the gap between the stage and the front row.

'And would you mind coming to the front?' she asked Callum.

'What for?' He looked nervous.

'It's really important,' Bryony answered. 'Please?'

Jasmine nudged him and Callum made his way down. He stopped near Bryony, and Mr Brook on the front row shot her a warning look. He was clearly still rattled about the mention of his toilets, and hated not being in control.

'Thanks, Callum,' Bryony whispered as Callum shuffled awkwardly. 'And don't worry.'

Bryony now went off to find Mr Thimblefold, sitting halfway back with Grandpa. She persuaded him down to the front too, and Grandpa went along for moral support.

The audience were spellbound. You could have heard a pin drop.

'Mr Thimblefold,' said Bryony, 'do you recognise this man?' She pointed at Callum Stepney.

Mr Thimblefold looked. He shook his head. 'Err, no. I don't thi—' But suddenly he stopped, almost as if a street light had just flickered on in his brain.

'Oh, wait!' gasped Mr Thimblefold, peering through his small round spectacles. 'Why I do believe … yes – well, goodness me! *This* is the man I saw in the street – last Monday afternoon – through my window!'

'At what time?' asked Bryony.

'A few minutes after five. Just after the Brooks' silver was left in my shop.'

And at this the audience gave an audible gasp. 'Oooooo!'

Chapter 15

'Callum,' continued Bryony, 'last Monday afternoon, did you take a box of silver from Brook Dale Manor and leave it in Mr Thimblefold's shop?'

'Sure,' Callum nodded. 'I left it there for him to clean.'

Bryony started to pace like Ebony Swann – minus the tightrope, but you couldn't have everything.

'Ah, yes you did!' Bryony nodded. 'You knew they wanted it cleaned because you'd heard the Brooks *talking* about cleaning their silver, hadn't you?'

'Yeah,' Callum nodded. 'We all did. Me and Joe

and Pete. We all heard them when we was over there fixing them loos – which took *days*.'

'Hold on!' Mr Brook jumped up and marched over. '*I* didn't ask him to take my silver to be cleaned!'

'No, you didn't,' Bryony replied. 'You'd made your *own* plans instead, hadn't you? You were going to get that posh place in Pudding Lane to clean it for you. Those people – Cuthbert and Fig.'

'Yes! Yes! Quite so!' Mr Brook nodded. 'But how do you know about *them*?!'

'I . . . just . . . do,' Bryony answered, glossing over the fact that she'd snooped around his study just seconds before she'd got herself locked in his loo!

The audience were open-mouthed. They were listening more intently than they'd actually done during the play!

'But the point is,' continued Bryony, '– um, Mr Cooper, where are you?'

Mr Cooper raised a hand. He was close to the back with his family, all sitting together.

'*The point,*' repeated Bryony, now raising her voice to make sure that no one missed this, 'is that Mr Cooper didn't steal the silver, and Mr

Thimblefold didn't take it from anyone – because Callum was *asked* to take the silver to Thimblefold's Trinkets and Treasures by the Brooks.'

'No!' yelled Mr Brook. 'I just told you I didn't ask him!'

'Um, nor me,' called Mrs Brook from the front row with a shrug.

'No – *you* didn't,' replied Bryony. 'Neither of you. But just like in *Cinderella*, if the shoe doesn't fit one – or even *two* – it doesn't mean that there's not another. For the Brook who asked Callum to take the box of silver ...'

Bryony paused like Miss Swann for dramatic effect.

'... was Georgina.'

Up on stage, Georgina now flew out of her sidecar. 'Daddy! I demand to go home right now! How *dare* she say things about me!'

'Quite right!' called Mr Brook, looking up at his daughter. 'This is all utter nonsense. Come, darling!'

'No – wait.'

Mrs Brook now stood up from her seat and walked up to Callum Stepney very calmly.

'*Did* Georgie ask you, Callum?' she asked.

The audience were entranced, missing their open mouths with fistfuls of popcorn and dropping it down their Christmas jumpers instead.

'Err, yeah,' Callum nodded. 'Georgina did ask and I took it for the trinket man to clean.'

'But you were *meant* to ask for *money*!' Georgina suddenly snapped, glaring down from the stage at Callum. 'I thought when I told you to take the silver, you'd realise I wanted you *to sell it*!'

The crowd gasped.

'Eh?' said Callum. He looked genuinely confused. 'I thought I was helping – just taking it to clean, not selling it.'

'And *that*,' said Bryony, turning to Georgina, 'is why you were so cross on Monday night at the stables. Amber had no idea where her brother was, did she? Or why you wanted him either. But you wanted him because you thought he'd run off with your money . . . *for the silver.*'

Georgina clapped a hand over her mouth, realising her angry outburst just now had landed her in heaps of trouble.

'Georgina!' cried Mr Brook.

'Why?' gasped her mother. 'Why ask him to take the silver, Georgina?'

But Georgina just folded her arms and stuck her nose in the air.

'The school ski trip, I'm guessing?' Bryony chipped in, her gaze not leaving Georgina.

Being locked in the Brooks' loo the day before yesterday had served its purpose after all. For there Bryony had heard with her own ears how desperate Georgina had been to go on the trip.

'But *everyone* was going,' Georgina hissed at Bryony. 'Not that *you'd* ever understand. Huh! I bet you've never been skiing in your life, whereas *I*,' cried Georgina, 'am really good at it! So I thought, okay – why—' But suddenly she stopped.

'. . . Why not sell the family silver and pay for the ski trip *yourself*?' Bryony finished Georgina's sentence for her.

'So what anyway?!' Georgina snapped. 'If you *think* about it, I did nothing wrong! It's the Brooks' family silver and *I* am a Brook, so I should get a say too. And *I* didn't want it cleaned – but sold, so there!'

'Georgina!' gasped Mrs Brook and even *Mr* Brook looked furious.

'It wasn't *yours* to do *anything* with!' he said.

He snapped his fingers. 'Home, young lady! And you can forget ski trips for a very long time, and any *other* treats come to that!'

Georgina looked outraged but stomped down the stage steps, her princess gown twinkling like crazy. She marched out of the door and her mother followed. Then, gathering up his coat, Mr Brook turned to leave too.

'Um, before you do . . .' Grandpa stepped forward. 'I think some folk deserve an apology from you.'

Grandpa invited the Coopers to come down and join him. They were reluctant, but the audience began calling for them too, kindly and warmly, until they came.

Meredith ran straight to hold Bryony's hand as Grandpa looked back at Mr Brook.

'These people,' said Grandpa, 'did nothing wrong. But you . . . you said that they did.'

'I . . .' Mr Brook swallowed hard as if he had a nasty taste in his mouth.

He turned to the Coopers. 'I . . . shouldn't have assumed that you . . . took my silver. So . . . well . . . I apologise.'

He went to leave again.

'Not so fast,' said Grandpa, and Mr Brook stopped.

'What now?!'

Grandpa gestured toward Mr Thimblefold.

'Him?' scowled Mr Brook.

Grandpa didn't answer.

'What am I apologising to *him* for?'

Mr Brook tilted his head to the side as if jiggling his thoughts might help him – momentarily – see things from another's perspective.

'Oh – *fine!*' he snarled, now turning to Mr Thimblefold.

'I am *sorry*,' said Mr Brook through gritted teeth, 'that your customers thought you an *old fraud*!'

'Because . . .' added Bryony bravely as Meredith watched her in awe.

'*Because* . . .' Mr Brook now clenched his fists, '. . . *you're not*.'

As if a play had finally finished, the hall was now filled with resounding applause.

'Hear hear!' boomed Miss Parsley. 'Now let's go and have mince pies!'

As the audience started leaving, Bryony's friends gathered round, all patting her on the back.

'Wow,' said Hari. 'Respect, Bry. That was one hard case to crack.'

'Brilliant!' smiled Emma. 'I knew you could do it!'

'But I couldn't have done it without *you* lot,' said Bryony. 'And I certainly wouldn't have spoken up on that stage without the rest of the Super Six right beside me.'

Josh nudged her. 'Come on, then! Time to go home and get ready for mince pies – I-I mean – carol singing!'

He grinned, and with a nod, his sister grinned back.

'Thanks, Bryony,' said Mr Cooper. And Meredith (and even Morgan) gave her the biggest of hugs.

Mr Thimblefold looked really grateful too, *and* he was smiling again!

'Yes, thank you!' he said. 'And your friends too. This really means so much to me. I shall open my little shop again right after Christmas. I've been missing it so much.'

'Before the 28th!' Bryony said quickly. 'There's a lady who wants the train clock for her son.'

Mr Thimblefold nodded. 'Oh, right! Well, I'll make sure of it.'

They headed out together, but suddenly they

stopped as the corridor was crammed with people. During the play the snow had really come down so they could barely get out through the door.

'The lanes will be right blocked!' Farmer Jenkins grumbled.

'Oh dear!' The postman shook his head. 'I'm afraid that's that for the Friendship Jars then. The roads were bad enough *before*, but no cars, or vans, including mine, will get anywhere now,' he said.

'Grrr, I'd take them in me tractor,' puffed Farmer Jenkins. ''Cept it's broke!'

There was a chorus of sad mutterings, then everyone fell silent. The Friendship Jars were such an important part of Christmas . . .

'Oh, wait! Hold your horses!' It was Miss Pigeon. 'I've just had a vision!' she cried. And as everyone gathered around to listen, out it tumbled as fast as the snow . . .

'I sees a jar – and another – and a little pony-reindeer! And *he* shall save Christmas or I's a silly sprout!' She spun round to Miss Parsley . . .

'Don't you DARE.'

*

'This is *such* a responsibility!' Bryony said. 'Are you sure you're okay with it, hmm?'

Red blinked back, his big brown eyes twinkling.

'Yes, of course you are!' Bryony beamed. 'Silly me to worry, eh? If anyone can save Christmas, Red – it's you!'

Miss Pigeon had had a vision of a red-nosed reindeer guiding Santa's sleigh through the snow. When Bryony had pointed out they didn't have a red-nosed reindeer, the old lady had told her to think harder. Then Bryony realised – the *red*-nosed reindeer in the vision had meant: Red!

Miss Pigeon and Bryony had then planned the whole thing, and Bryony had just shared the plan with Red. The whole town were now gathering at the Market Square to have carols and mince pies. Then the Friendship Jar Procession would be led by *Red* so everyone would get their Friendship Jars under the tree!

As Bryony rode Red to the school to collect the jars she was wondering what his sleigh would look like. Miss Pigeon had said to leave that bit to her.

'Nearly there!' Bryony felt almost dizzy with

excitement as they turned up Chestnut Lane. And there it was, in front of the school gates.

'Oh, Red!' cried Bryony. Miss P had chosen so well – for the Coopers' little caravan made the loveliest sleigh she'd ever seen!

It had been loaded with all the Friendship Jars, and Blossom was ready to pull it. But Red was going to be Blossom's guiding reindeer!

'And *look* – there's Santa!' Bryony gasped. Miss Pigeon hadn't told her *this* part of the plan either. But what a lovely surprise! For sitting, all ready to drive the sleigh, was *Mr Thimblefold* in his big red duffle coat! His long white beard was glistening with snowflakes and his eyes behind his spectacles shone bright. He was also wearing his best polar bear bow tie which looked adorable.

'Bryony!' called Josh. He came running up the lane. Behind him were the others riding their ponies, who were all wearing little elf hats: pink for Princess Perla, yellow for little Daffy, mint green for Tor and blue for Piggy. They looked such a picture!

'And this is for Red!' Josh hurried up and clipped a set of antlers into his mane.

241

'I customised them for him, see?' Josh smiled. 'So they won't slip over his eyes.'

'Thanks, Josh!' said Bryony. Then she patted Red.

'Right! Let's get Christmas started!'

As Red led the procession down the town's main street, snow was falling softly, the lamps were all lit and the brass band was playing 'We Wish You a Merry Christmas'!

Bryony had never felt prouder of him, guiding Blossom and Mr Thimblefold to the tree, her friends on their ponies all bringing up the rear, like happy little elves!

The Friendship Jars were then all unloaded and the mince pies passed around. As Bryony ate hers, she looked up at the sky. The moon was huge and silvery, and there was magic in the air. Then suddenly she felt a small hand patting her back.

Bryony turned. 'Oh, Meredith!' she said.

'Thanks for our Friendship Jar!' grinned Meredith.

'Wait! How did you know it was me?' asked Bryony as the rest of the Coopers appeared.

'Well, the best friend we've had since coming has been *you*,' Mrs Cooper said with a smile.

'So we guessed!' cried Morgan. 'Are we right?'

Bryony nodded. 'Very good detective work!' she smiled.

'And *wait*!' squealed Meredith, taking a shoebox off her dad and handing it to Bryony.

'Open it!' cried Morgan, so carefully she took off the lid.

Bryony gasped – for snuggled under a small knitted blanket was Hector the moon gazing hare!

'I told Dad to keep him for you,' said Meredith, 'the *very* first day I met you!'

'It's the longest she's ever kept a secret!' Mr Cooper laughed.

'But I can't ... I mean ...' Bryony shook her head. 'I've spent all the money I'd saved.'

'No, no!' said Mr Cooper. 'See, this is a gift. From our family to yours.'

Bryony beamed. 'Wow! Thank you all so much!' Now Mum would have the most adorable gift, one that Bryony knew she would love. And Hector could tell little broken Selena how the moon looked every night, while *she* could report on the moonlit lawn and all the animals who plodded by!

243

The whole town was singing and snow was falling softly as Bryony went back to her beautiful Red being held by Grandpa near the Christmas tree. Little children were patting the special pony-reindeer who had guided Santa's sleigh so beautifully.

'Ah, Red,' said Bryony quietly. 'You're quite the celebrity, I see!'

But Red only had eyes for Bryony now, and he gently nuzzled her shoulder.

'Happy Christmas to you too,' Bryony whispered back, gazing up to the stars.

With friends, and family – and Red by her side – there was *no* place quite like Brook Dale at Christmas . . .

Who's Your Perfect Pony Pal?

1

What's your favourite way to spend a day?

- **A** Messing about with mates in the garden
- **B** Out on your bike having adventures
- **C** Doing some craft in your bedroom

2

Your friends would describe you as:

- **A** Funny
- **B** Adventurous
- **C** Careful

What animal would you be?

- **A** A playful puppy
- **B** A beautiful cat
- **C** A tortoise – plus shell for 'quiet time'

In a café you would pick:

A A huge ice-cream sundae – with EVERYTHING

B Something you've never tried before

C Always cupcakes (you know you like them!)

What's your favourite way to travel?

A Pogo stick

B Aeroplane

C On foot

Your friend is upset, so you would...

A Make them laugh

B Listen

C Get upset too

If you had a magical power, it would be...

A Changing colour with a sneeze

B Reading people's minds

C Invisibility

Your Perfect Pony Pal is Daffodil!

You're so much fun – just like playful Daffy, and you LOVE being on the go. You make others laugh, even if you sometimes act first and think later! You've quite the sunniest of personalities and are brimming with surprises. You light up any room by just being you!

Your Perfect Pony Pal is Red!

Like Red, you love adventure, but you're kind and caring too. You consider other people's feelings, and you're a loyal friend and great listener. You like to please others and you have TONS of sparkle. You're always the first there in a crisis and are completely dependable. Go, you!

Your Perfect Pony Pal is Tornado!

Just like Tor, you're creative and thoughtful. But others shouldn't be fooled, for under a shy exterior you've *bags* of bravery. A solid friend, you'll never tell others what to do, and no one cares like you. You're amazing! Truly.

Now you need to *believe* it!

Make a Festive Pony Decoration!

You will need:

- Tracing paper
- Pencil
- Piece of card, about 11 cm square
- Pair of scissors
- Hole punch
- Piece of ribbon, about 22 cm long

What to do:

1. Place tracing paper on top of the pony template (see over page) and draw around the shape.
2. Cut out your tracing.
3. Place your traced pony on to the piece of card and draw around it. Then carefully cut it out.
4. Using a hole punch, make a hole in your cardboard pony on top of its back.
5. Thread ribbon or string through this hole and tie the ends to make a hanging loop.
6. Decorate your pony with glitter, or colour with pencils.
7. Hang your festive pony on the Christmas tree or in your window.